D1130538

THE BOOK OF
DREAMS

THE BOOK OF DREAMS

Edited by Nick Gevers

ORIGINAL STORIES BY

Robert Silverberg
Lucius Shepard
Jay Lake
Kage Baker
Jeffrey Ford

Illustration by J. K. Potter

SUBTERRANEAN PRESS 2010

First Edition

ISBN
978-1-59606-284-9

Subterranean Press
PO Box 190106
Burton, MI 48519

www.subterraneanpress.com

TABLE OF CONTENTS

THE PRISONER

ROBERT SILVERBERG

LATELY his dreams have had great urgency. He is sprinting frantically up some bright windy beach from the edge of the surf, the cold rising tide licking at his heels, desperately trying to reach the dark rockpile at the foot of the nearby cliff where he can clamber up above the rapidly rising water. Or he is jogging through some nasty wasteland of spongy yellowish soil while narrow serpentine heads rise all about him out of little circular craters, snapping at his ankles with angry fangs. Or he is running uphill on a broad, steep urban boulevard, dodging the speeding cars that come rocketing downhill toward him.

He awakens from these dreams sweaty, panting, shivering with residual fear. They are only dreams, he tells himself, as he showers and shaves and dresses for work. They are strange dreams, they are unpleasant dreams, they are *very* unpleasant dreams, but all they are is dreams, after all, mere effluvia of the night, and they will fade and be gone swiftly in the bright light of morning.

The strange thing, though, is that they *don't* fade.

Through the first hour of the day's work they seem more real than the work itself. He stares into his screen and sees, not the gaily colored charts and graphs of the corporate ebb and flow, but the menacing images he thought he had left behind at the coming of dawn. Bristly antennae, slavering jaws, bulging green eyes, great jagged rocks bouncing down a hillside toward him, a roaring river in full spate above a dangling fractured bridge— whatever ugly terrifying scene had intruded on his sleeping mind the night before carries over into the day and churns and mills before him like some ghastly movie that has seized possession of his terminal.

His distress shows on his face. "Are you okay?" they ask. Or they say, "Big night out last night?" Or sometimes it is, "I'm beginning to think you're taking this job too seriously, Dave."

To which he replies such things as, "Bit of a headache this morning," or, "I look that bad, do I?" or, more usually, "No, really, I'm fine. Really."

But what they see is what there is. The face that looks back at him from the washroom mirror is unquestionably pale, haggard, tense. He splashes himself with cold water, briskly rubs the muscles of his cheeks and forehead to relax them, pulls his lips back in an idiotic forced grin that he hopes will seep inward so that he looks more at ease. Usually by lunchtime everything is normal again. He goes out with the gang, he does the standard banter, he swaps movie comments and sports chitchat and stock predictions, and when he returns to the office the face in the washroom mirror is his ordinary everyday face again.

But then, come night—

It is two years and some months since his marriage broke up, and though he began going out again quickly enough afterward, he usually spends most nights of the week except Friday and Saturday alone. Which means that when dreams arrive, and if they are horrific ones, the sort of dreams that are beginning to become the norm for him, he has only his pillow to reach to for comfort when the sweaty anguish awakens him. Just as well, perhaps: More than once recently he has terrified some new Saturday-night companion with the four a.m. scream and clutch, which he has found is a good way of transforming a promising new relationship into a one-night stand. "Sorry," he will say. "That was one lulu of a bad dream."

"It must have been," she says, and he can tell from her tone that she is already thinking of how soon she can get her clothes on and head for home.

Everybody dreams, he tells himself, and everybody has a nightmare once in a while. What he's going through now is a little unusual, perhaps, an odd spate of spectacularly grim stuff. But just a phase, he thinks. Maybe a temporary metabolic upheaval, or some short-lived digestive strangeness, a delayed reaction to the breakup of his marriage, or maybe some oblique reflection of ongoing challenges at the office. It will pass. It will pass. Meanwhile he has started to dread going to sleep.

AFTER THREE weeks he shares his troubles with Charlie, who is plump and balding and calm and likes to play the role of father confessor and amateur shrink around the office. Charlie has been through a lot of stuff himself, and he has read a lot of books, and he is the quickest hand anyone has seen at dredging up an Internet diagnosis for any sort of ailment.

"It's a normal biological process, dreaming," Charlie says. "The nocturnal shedding of daily stress through transformation of negative energy into randomly created imagery: a catharsis, a cleansing. We need the dreaming process in order to stay sane. You must be working your way through a lot of inner crap, things stored on some level that isn't even consciously accessible to you."

"And turning them into a nightly horror flick?"

"It's no use trying to understand the workings of your unconscious mind, Dave. There's no logic to it. It's not a rational entity. Almost by definition, what it pushes up into view passeth all understanding."

"But Freud—"

"Freud was a pioneer, and pioneers by definition don't know where the hell they're going. Columbus thought he'd landed in the Indies, remember? But they turned out to be the *West* Indies. What Freud said about dreams a hundred years ago was all well and good in its day, but it's not the last word on the subject. It's pretty much the *first* word."

"These dreams are disgusting. Appalling. Loathsome."

"So?"

"They're emerging out of my own mind. And they're the sickest, most revolting things. Charlie, I feel *ashamed* to be having dreams like that."

"Ashamed? Of what?"

"That I could be generating such garbage. That I could be capable of imagining things like that. How can I not take responsibility for that? These are my dreams, these hideous things, the products of my own personal mind, as much my own creation as a novelist's novel or a composer's song or a playwright's play is."

"Wrong. You're trying to compare art—conscious, dedicated craftsmanship—with the muck that comes drifting randomly up out of the sewers of your mind."

"Randomly? Freud said—"

"I told you: Screw Freud," said Charlie. "Freud didn't know jack. It's all random. You aren't inventing this stuff, you're simply having it dumped on you by some impersonal inner force while you lie there asleep and defenseless. Why blame yourself for it? That's like somebody blaming himself for having cancer. For Christ's sake, you don't need to take responsibility for the flavor of your dreams. Isn't real life rough enough? Dave, there's no sense whatsoever beating yourself up over what goes on in your head when you aren't even conscious."

HE IS walking a tightrope stretching from one great midtown tower to another, eighty-odd floors above the ground. He knows that there is a crowd of people watching him from below, hundreds of people, maybe thousands, though he dares not look down. It is a cool sunny day, crisp and dry, and a brisk wind is blowing. He can feel the tightrope quivering against his bare feet. He has never done anything remotely like this before, and yet it was with great assurance that he had stepped out onto the rope, clutching his balance-pole lightly against his chest. At first it was easy. One step, another, another—

He realizes he is terrified. Nothing surprising about that; and yet he had felt no fear at the outset, and only now, perhaps a third of the way across, where he has gone too far to turn back, when it would be even more difficult to return to his starting point than to continue on to the opposite tower, do great sickening spasms of terror go curling upward through his body.

Keep going. Step. Step. Step. The rope sways. He adjusts his balance with the pole. Step. Step. Step. Yes! He is halfway across, now. Step. Step. He has never been so frightened in his life; but, then, he has never done anything as crazy as this before. And he is starting to think there's a chance he will make it. Step! Step! Step!

"Hey, schmuck!" calls a raucous voice from the roof of the tower behind him. "Schmuck, look at me!" And, like a schmuck, he does, twisting around and glancing

up over his shoulder, and sways and grabs air and topples, and topples, and topples, and the pavement comes
swooping up to meet him.

•‖———————‖•

HE BEGINS to keep a diary of the dreams, searching
for some common denominator in these calamitous sce-
narios. There is always danger in them, of course. Tension,
dread, suspense. He is in dire peril. Each night he finds
himself in some stark situation not of his own making,
where external forces threaten to snuff him out. He has
been out boating on the bay, and is swept overboard and
carried out to sea, and bobs, alone in the cold trackless
waters, unable even to see the shore, let alone reach it. He
is hiking in the woods, disturbs a branch, is seized in the
jaws of some remorseless metal trap. He is being frog-
marched through the streets with a jeering mob swarm-
ing on both sides of him, led to a plaza where a stake
and a great pile of logs and straw awaits him, and then a
crackling blaze—

The rack—the thumbscrew—the garrote—

He draws elaborate structural diagrams of the
dreams. He makes charts. He devotes evening after evening to their analysis. He is an educated, thoughtful man,
though his life has not worked out quite the way he had
expected. His daily work is trivial and it bores him, but it
is *his* work, and without it he would long ago have been
lost. These days it is his bulwark against the nightly mysterious assault of these dreams. And now he applies the

same sort of analytic techniques to the dreams that he uses each day in the office to sort and classify and draw conclusions from the information that he is paid to sort and classify and draw conclusions from.

An interesting pattern begins to emerge. He tells Charlie about it, his one confidante.

"It's starting to become clear," he says, "that I'm dreaming, not about myself, but about someone else. I'm not the protagonist—the victim—in all these various grisly events, but just a spectator. I'm there, I'm plenty scared, but I'm not actually the one in jeopardy. I'm just standing to one side, watching, like somebody at a movie."

Charlie is puzzled. "Really? Are you sure of that?"

"Sure? I'm not sure of anything. But that's how it starts to look as I write up my summaries of what I'm experiencing."

And he explains that as he replays each nightmare in his mind he has discovered that he has in fact displaced the center of the event. "We always assume that the central figure in our dreams, the consciousness through whom the dream is communicated to us, is ourself. We see him moving about before our mind's eye like an actor on a screen, but we attach our own identity to him, so that we are both watcher and performer. But that isn't actually how it is for me in these things."

It only *feels* to him, he says, as though he is the man desperately trying to outrun the rising tide, that he is the tottering trembler on the tightrope, that he is the panicky zigzagger darting between the traffic on that steep urban boulevard. In fact he has come to realize, as his analysis of the material proceeds, that he is merely looking on from one side, a witness to the sufferings of someone else.

Charlie is doubtful. Charlie still believes that when we dream, we dream about ourselves, even though we may think we are dreaming about someone else. For a man who has blown off Freud as not knowing jack, Charlie suddenly starts to seem very conventional indeed in his theory of dreams.

He decides not to argue the point. Let Charlie believe whatever he wants to believe. He has faith in his own analysis, and that faith grows stronger the longer he works with the material.

Of course there is no way for him to re-experience any one dream. None of the nightmares ever recurs in identical form; there is always a fresh one to torment him by night. But they remain with him as memories, all-too-vivid memories, and as he sets down synopses of them in his growing diary he starts to become more convinced than ever that his presence in each dream is in the role of an onlooker rather than a participant.

He was not the tightrope-walker; he may have been the man who shouted distractingly from the rooftop. He was not the man burned at the stake; he was somewhere in the midst of that jeering mob. He was not the drowning swimmer lost in the pathless expanse of a cold ocean; he was an observer floating somewhere high overhead, watching that bobbing head amongst the waves. In each dream the true protagonist is someone else, a hapless prisoner trapped in some extreme and frightening circumstance, and he himself is merely looking on.

Does that matter? The dreams are terrifying whether or not he perceives them as being about someone else's travail. The man in the dreams may be suffering terrible torment, but he is the one who awakens shaking with fear.

THE DAYS go by, and the nights, and nothing changes for the better. The man in the dreams has died a hundred horrible deaths, but is always restored to life in time for the next night's pitiless horrors.

HE—OR IS it the unknown *he?*—is in a tiny stone-walled prison chamber in which he can neither sit nor lie down nor stand, but must remain in a sort of half-crouch against the rough clammy wall, his frozen knees screaming, his knotted back writhing perpetually in pain, and here he must huddle, month after month, year after year, with no hope of release.

HE IS in the intensive care unit, with a feeding tube in his stomach and a mechanical ventilator operating his lungs, and he is surrounded by a webwork of intravenous piping that feeds him sedatives, narcotics, anesthetics. The glittering-eyed diabolical nurse is ratcheting the flow higher, higher, higher. His brain is swimming in a chemical bath. His mind is starting to blur. He lifts one hand—struggles feebly to signal for help—

HE IS in the most comfortable of beds in the most luxurious of hotels. But as he awaits sleep the bedclothes turn into writhing tentacles and wrap themselves around his wrists and ankles, pinning him down. He lies there spread-eagled, helpless, and the ceiling slowly begins to descend. He tries to scream, but no sound will emerge, and all he can do is wait, eyes ablaze with dread, as that inexorable mass glides serenely down to crush him.

HE IS driving swiftly up a freeway entrance ramp, with another car beside him to the right, and a third car materializes abruptly, coming *down* the freeway ramp toward them both. The third car is moving swiftly, but nevertheless it takes hours for it to descend the ramp, the cars unable to turn from their courses, each driver looking at the other two in a sort of stasis, until at last there is the screech of brakes and the immense sound of metal hitting metal in the moment of impact.

ALL ABOUT him are the low squalid buildings of some medieval city. A scaffold has been erected against a rough brick wall at one side of a great public square. An expectant crowd watches as he ascends the scaffold, kneels, fights off the moment of panic that rises suddenly within him, sweeps his long hair back, and places his head on the block. The headsman lifts his shining axe—

•╫────╫•

A NEW theme now emerges. The man is not only in some horrible peril; he is calling actively for help. There comes a dream in which he—or *he*—is hurrying down the platform of a railway station toward a waiting train, and the train's door closes in his face just as he reaches it, and he thrusts his hand through the door, trying to wrench it apart again. And he is caught, trapped, and as the train begins to move he is carried along down the platform, unable to pull his arm free; and as he comes to comprehend his predicament and looks about him in shock, crying out to the others on the platform for aid, another man in a red sweatshirt appears from somewhere and runs alongside him, tugging at his arm, trying to help. But there is nothing he can do and at the platform's end he steps sadly back, watching in dull shock as the figure caught in the door is swept away to be battered to death against the walls of the railway tunnel a few hundred yards down the track.

He recognizes that red sweatshirt. It belongs to him, an old and familiar garment.

Then, another night, he sees a figure standing on a narrow ledge that runs along the outer wall of a lofty apartment building. Somehow the man has gone out on the ledge and now is trying to find his way back inside, but all the windows are closed to him, and he edges slowly along, clutching the brickwork with his fingertips to support himself and shunting his feet sideways inch by inch, moving along the building's facade, going to window after window, apartment after apartment, and suddenly they are looking at each other, face to face, the man on the ledge outside and the man within, and the eyes of the man outside are wide with terror and in them can be seen the mute appeal, *Help me, help me, help me.*

It is his own apartment building. Just such a ledge runs the length of the building on the sixth floor. But he is not the man outside. He is the onlooker within.

And on still another night the dream-figure is stranded on the icy white slope of a vast mountain, some Alp, some Himalayan peak, with a giant crevasse yawning behind him and another beginning to open just ahead, and the ice rumbling and cracking almost beneath his feet, and the first hints of an impending avalanche overhead; and he looks imploringly across the crevasse, gesturing toward someone who perhaps can toss him a rope, but who is either unable or unwilling to do it. And also he is looking back across that crevasse from the other side.

There is no mistaking that pleading look. He has seen it three times, at least, now. Quite probably he has failed to see it in earlier visitations, but it was there. He is certain now that the man in the dream is looking outward toward him across the wall of sleep, to him specifically, begging for rescue.

Help me. Help me. Help me.

"WHAT CAN I do?" he asks Charlie. "How can I help him?"

But Charlie is beginning to lose interest in the whole problem. "You can't," he says, dismissively. "He doesn't exist. He's just a projection of yourself. In these dreams you've simply divided yourself in two, a watcher and a sufferer, but they're both the same person."

"I don't think so."

"What can I say? These are your dreams. He's a figment of your imagination. You want to believe he's someone else, well, okay, then he's somebody else. If you want to help him, reach in and pull him out, okay?"

THE DREAMS do not let up. And he begins to understand that the world of dreams is another world, one that exists beside our own—a world where nothing is real and everything is possible. He has been staring into that world every night of his life without knowing what it is.

He is certain now, with the sort of strange certainty that comes in dreams, that the man in the dreams is a real person, trapped in that other world the way one of the dream-figures had become trapped on the ledge of that building, the way another had been seized by the door of that train. And he is sending messages asking for help.

How could he ignore that call? He sees that it is his task to reach into the other world and pull that poor sufferer forth, just as Charlie had jokingly suggested, or he will never have a night's peace again himself.

Mon semblable,—mon frere!

He had never been a particularly compassionate man—that may have been one of the reasons for the breakup of his marriage—but, chilly and aloof though he often was, he had never refused aid to someone in trouble. It was his saving grace.

He will not refuse now. He will offer help.

But how? How?

•‖———‖•

HE TELLS himself, as he makes ready for bed, that when that night's dreams come, he will do everything he can to initiate contact, to extend a hand across the border between the one world and the other.

Tonight the dream-figure is stumbling across an endless Sahara, tongue thick and blackened with thirst, eyes wild. He is plainly at the end of his endurance. Just beyond the next dune lies a fertile green oasis, but he lacks the strength to get there.

Keep going! *Come on—come on—just a little way more!*

No use. The man staggers, stumbles, falls face-forward into the hot sands.

And on another night he is lost in a city where the streets melt and flow before him as he walks, substantial avenues turning to water, great thoroughfares becoming flaccid ropy masses of dough. He knows he must get to the other side of the city before nightfall—the welfare of someone precious to him depends on it—but he can make no progress; all is fluid and indeterminate. He pauses, contemplating the possibility of some more stable route that would take him to his goal, and indeed the dreaming observer knows that there is such a route, just a few blocks ahead, but when he calls out to tell him that, the words are swept away by the wind. And as he stands there the pavement begins to move beneath his feet and he is swept backward as though by a relentless river. Darkness begins to descend; the city vanishes; he is swept by the wildest terror.

<hr />

HIS REAL life, such as it had been, has nearly vanished altogether. He rises at the same hour as always, but instead of looking at the newspaper or watching the morning news he transcribes his notes on the night's dreams. He eats the same breakfast as ever, without tasting his food. He goes to the office by the usual route and does his work mechanically, competently, no more and no less engaged with it than he had ever been. During the lunch break he generally stays at his desk and eats a sandwich. He has almost no contact with his fellow workers. Charlie, plainly aware that something is amiss, comes over to inquire about the state of his health, but he replies with a shrug and a vague smile.

"Still having nightmares?" Charlie asks.

"Sometimes," he says.

He has stopped calling the few women he had been seeing. None of them call him. Just as well: Even though he no longer awakens screaming from his darker dreams, now that they have become such a customary part of his existence, it would be a distraction to have someone lying beside him in bed at night. He wants to focus all his attention on the dreams themselves.

The thing to do, he has decided, is to try to re-dream one of the dreams he has already had, particularly one in which the dream-figure is obviously pleading for help. Since the scenario of the dream is already known to him, like the plot of some movie he has seen before, he believes that he will be able to intervene sooner, at some point where the situation has not yet become irrevocably catastrophic, and offer the dream-figure the succor he needs. The window-ledge dream, he thinks, would be a particularly fruitful one to employ. To be able to go immediately to the right window, to open it, to pull the man through to safety.

But deliberately to recapitulate some already dreamed dream is not such an easy thing to accomplish. In the hour before bedtime he lets his mind dwell on the images he hopes to conjure up; he goes to his own window-ledge, runs his hand along it, measures its width, imagines what it would be like to climb out onto it right now and sidle along the face of the building. Then, closing his eyes, he pictures the tormented figure he had seen out there, the frightened man despairingly struggling to keep his balance as he inches along. The picture is a vivid one. He can almost even make out the features of the man's face, something that he has not really succeeded in doing before: He thinks he has an idea of what the dream-figure's face looks like, he is certain that it is the same man in each and every dream, but the specific details elude him when he tries to describe them to himself. He could not have drawn a sketch of his face, nor even responded usefully to the expert questions of some police-department artist trying to guide him toward a description. Yet in these rehearsals for sleep it seems to him that he has envisioned the face in essence if not in specifics, that with only a little more effort he could come to see it clearly.

As he waits for sleep he keeps the window-ledge scene in mind; but when he drops off—and it has been taking him longer and longer to fall asleep each night—some other dream always comes, some dream of jeopardy, of course, but always a new one, as though the supply of these nightmares is infinite and none will ever recur. He is caught by surprise each time by the new surroundings in which the dream is set, unable to move himself into the right position to be helpful, unable to take the necessary steps to effect the desired rescue.

A month goes by, two, three. The sunny days of summer give way to the first rains of autumn.

And then, one night, the dream-state comes over him moments after he reaches his pillow and he realizes that at last he has been granted the recurrence of a dream. It is one in which the man is floating in a huge bottom-less pool of chilly black water, unable to direct his own movements, simply drifting helplessly from one side to another across the face of that watery abyss like some bit of flotsam while sleek glossy monsters of the deep with gaping jaws and yellow eyes circle hungrily about him, closing in for the kill.

This is not a new dream. He has had it before, and he knows exactly what he must do. There is a stout coil of rope lying in a neat stack on the far side of the pool. The last time he dreamed this dream, the rope had been there also but he had simply remained where he was, watching as though in a stupor as the beasts unhurriedly closed in, surrounded their victim, toyed with him, and finally, in a frenzy of thrashing flukes, fell upon him and devoured him. This time he fights away that stupor. He wills himself around to the other side of the pool, crossing the great distance separating him from it with the speed of thought, and seizes one end of the coil of rope in a tight grasp, and, pivoting sharply, flings the other end far into the water.

"Quick!" he calls. "Grab hold of it!"

The man in the pool looks up, startled. Sees the rope; swims to it and seizes it; lets himself be drawn toward the edge of the pool. The man standing on the shore has no doubt of the other's face, now. The features are his own.

He reels the other in.

"Here," he says, kneeling by the water's edge, reaching his free hand down toward the other.

He extends his hand into that dark abyss, makes contact, grips and braces himself and pulls. Yanking with all his strength, he draws the other to him, draws him up and out and *through*, and in that same moment he feels a snap and a twist and a twirl of reciprocity, as though he is standing upon a moving turntable that is swinging him around into the mysterious realm beyond. He struggles to resist the force that is catapulting him onward; but resistance is impossible. He is powerless against such unyielding pressure. He is hurled through that invisible wall.

•H————————H•

ON THE far side he finds himself alone in a soundless world.

And then he is sprinting frantically up some bright windy beach from the edge of the surf, the cold rising tide licking at his heels, desperately trying to reach the dark rockpile at the foot of the nearby cliff where he can clamber up above the rapidly rising water.

DREAM BURGERS
AT THE MOUTH OF HELL

LUCIUS SHEPARD

HIS long, handsome face is tanned brown as apple butter and the lines on it, nicks at the corners of the eyes
and mouth, look placed there by design, like decorative
sprays etched on Navaho silver. It's a face without a dis-
cernable trace of human character and is most adept at
expressing a homogenized blend of abiding concern and
sincerity that may be familiar to those who have formed
childhood associations with sexual deviants and/or
Baptist preachers. His blue-gray eyes bulge faintly—they
have the lustrous convexity of those opaque glass bricks
that adorn the entranceways to certain 1940s Hollywood
bungalows—and when he turns your way, the air seems to
ripple with his unearthly stare, giving rise to the suspicion

that some sort of science-fiction bug creature is peering at you from within a cleverly wrought disguise of Armani and human skin and plastic hair with the sheen of polished jet. The creature's name is Marshall ("Mars" to his intimates) Ziegler and, according to a recent *Forbes* article, he is the eleventh most powerful person in the movie industry, the head of Virtual Light Productions, a subsidiary of Dreamworks.

Ziegler, then, pulls his silver-and-blue Bugatti Veyron to the curb at the corner of Sunset and Gower, where a tall, disheveled manchild in sport coat, polo shirt and jeans, Arthur Embry, stands with hands in his pockets, gazing with a vacant expression that his friends might recognize as longing at Roscoe's House of Chicken and Waffles, debating whether to save a couple of bucks and opt for the Oscar (wings and waffles) or go all-out and blow eleven-ninety on the Lord Harvey platter. The Bugatti's horn (an annoying special effect that digitally emulates a panther's snarl) ripsaws the air. Startled, Embry takes a backward step and bumps into a Mexican transsexual with a stormy yet kittenish face, who curses him roundly in her mother tongue before returning to dickering over price and services with a pasty, balding muppet wearing a Celine Dion concert tee.

"Embry," says Ziegler, peering over the top of his Moss Lipow shades. "Right?"

Confused, because Ziegler has never before noticed him, let alone spoken, Embry says, "Unh."

"You eaten?" Ziegler asks.

Embry waves at Roscoe's and starts to speak.

"Come on." Ziegler pushes open the passenger door. "Break bread with me."

Cinderella stepping into her pumpkin coach, Embry thinks, likely felt this blessed, this vulnerable.

The Bugatti surges away from the curb before he can close the door, acceleration pressing him into supple leather that reeks of new car smell. Unable to come up with a witty conversation-starter, Embry says, "New car, huh?"

"It's not the car," Ziegler says, downshifting. "It's me...my cologne. I figured everybody loves that smell, so I asked my cologne guy to whip something up that'd make me smell that way."

"Oh."

"You know what makes that smell?"

"No, I don't," Embry says, wondering how it feels to have a "cologne guy".

"Pthalates. Chemicals they use to seal the plastic parts of the interior. They're fucking carcinogens. The same shit basically that gets glue-sniffers off. That's why people love it. Because it gives them a buzz." Ziegler shifts again as he pulls onto the freeway. "When my guy tells me that, I say for him to go ahead and whip me up some. I'm thinking if people are getting a buzz off me, it gives me an edge in business. I got great health insurance and I'm not going to sweat a little cancer."

Embry, imagining how it must feel to have great health insurance, says, "Uh-huh."

Ziegler punches a stud on the gearbox and the roof retracts with a series of well-lubricated clicks and hums that make it seem the car is having sex with itself.

"Ray Dressler tells me you're going to do a couple of drafts of the dragon picture."

"Yup," says Embry, essaying a breezy informality.

Ziegler looks at him askance. "Ever see a dragon?"

"I saw the original picture of course. *Dragonslayer.* And I've…"

"I asked if you'd ever seen a dragon."

"Uh, you mean…a real one?"

Ziegler snorts as though amused. "Right!"

THEY DRIVE south toward Long Beach or maybe Palos Verdes, their destination (Embry imagines) a sanctuary of the privileged where naked demimondes serve peacock tits glacé and liquor made from laurel leaves to what passes for the Hollywood aristocracy; but Ziegler turns off the freeway at the Whittier exit and heads into the barrens that border City of Industry, tracts of unexploited real estate, mainly denuded yellowish brown hills and fields. In the midst of a field stitched by a row of high tension towers, approached via a dust-blown strip of asphalt, sits a retro-style diner sheathed in aluminum and so dazzled by the sun that at certain angles it resembles the white-hot heart of an explosion. Embry's disappointed, but then he notices that a vintage Cadillac El Dorado is probably the least expensive car parked alongside it. The diner, he reasons, must be one of those working class joints renowned for its burgers or pies or chicken mole that have been "discovered" by celebrities and thereafter enjoy a season or two of exclusivity before becoming an attraction for Japanese tour groups. He's forced to modify this thesis, however, on seeing the door. Constructed of planks blackened with age; the crossbeams held in place by wooden pegs; with brass Gothic letters at eye level announcing that this is The Mouth Of Hell: It's such a relic, you'd expect to encounter a decorating scheme incorporating spider webs and medieval torture devices within; but although the interior is more spacious than most diners and the soft post-rock music that's playing isn't what you would expect, nothing seems out of the ordinary—a formica counter, stools, and sparkly red vinyl booths, the majority occupied by well-dressed middle-aged men (including several Embry recognizes from award show telecasts) and showy young women who eye-fuck Ziegler as he makes his entrance, a few of them sending perfunctory smiles Embry's way in case he turns out to be somebody.

Ziegler takes possession of a horseshoe-shaped corner booth that could easily hold seven or eight people and affords Embry a view of an adjoining table at which an aging actress noshes on a salad and holds a one-sided conversation with a young man who, judging by his kicked-dog reactions, is either her boy toy or a publicity flack. A waitress appears, bearing menus. She's just his type: tall, fresh-faced and college girl pretty, slender, dark brown hair, wearing a forest green uniform with Mouth of Hell in flaming letters stitched across the left breast pocket. The only flaw he notices (and he feels with time that this might not be perceived as a flaw, but as an accent to perfection) is an overly large set of front teeth that, although white and straight, produce a considerable overbite. He finds he's beaming like an idiot at Sue (the name stitched on her right breast pocket), possessed by a feeling of well-being that grows increasingly pronounced moment by moment. Sue starts to deal out the menus, but Ziegler holds up a palm and, with an imperious air, says, "Mister Embry will have a couple of Dreamburgers and a shake." He looks to Embry. "Chocolate good?"

"Yeah, sure."

"And I..." Ziegler ponders. "I'll have the Belgian waffle and coffee."

"How you want those Dreamburgers?"

Embry drags his gaze up from Sue's pockets and makes contact with doe eyes fringed by long, delicate lashes. "Medium," he says dazedly.

"Done deal!"

She flashes her grille and goes behind the counter to pass their order back to the kitchen; then she snags two plates and delivers them to another booth. Watching her calf muscles bunch and uncoil, Embry's reminded of an old girlfriend in New York City (once his home) who had a similar walk and, for that matter, a similar overbite, a sexual naïf of thirty years whom he educated in the ways of Eros and who proved to be a natural submissive, eventually dumping him for a guy with his own dungeon. Recalling heartbreak, Embry chuckles.

"Feeling kind of spacey?" Ziegler asks.

No longer tense, Embry rests his arm on the back of the booth and stretches out a leg on the seat. "Yeah, little bit."

"It's the drugs," says Ziegler. "They hit you with an aerosol when you enter. Psilocybin, MDA, a jolt of THC. By the time your food's ready, you're ready to eat, let me tell you."

Embry searches Ziegler's empty face for signs that he's being put on.

"Scout's honor." Ziegler gives the two-finger salute that boys across America once gave to signify their allegiance to an outmoded moral code. "The air, the food and drink...it's all drugged. Don't worry. Every once in a while somebody slips off their track, but that hardly ever happens. The cook's a master chemist. You'll eat, you'll have an experience, and after that you'll be good to go back to work."

"What kind of experience?"

Ziegler waves at someone in another booth. "I've got to talk with this guy a minute."

He slides out into the aisle, leaving Embry to be entranced by the dancing sparkles on the red vinyl, to see in the gleaming cutlery (nudged from its orderly rank by his elbow) a character from the *I Ching*, and to stare out the picture window at an approaching car, a dark blue Honda making its way out of a cloud of dust and exhaust toward the Mouth of Hell…and then, scarcely a hundred feet away, dematerializing like a shuttle in the grip of a transporter beam. Embry gapes at the ghost image of the Honda as it fades from sight and gives a start when Sue reappears and says, "Sorry about that. I'll give Security a call."

Embry's voice is tinged with hysteria. "The car…it fucking vanished!"

"Oh!" Sue puts a hand to her mouth. "Is this your first time? It is, isn't it? See, they're supposed to scan the cars at the turn-off and do the transfer then."

"I beg your pardon?"

"Okay." She sets a chocolate milkshake on the table. "When Security spots someone inappropriate take the turn to the diner, they…"

"Inappropriate?"

"If they're not a member or the guest of a member. When Security spots, you know, a Honda?" She laughs. "I mean none of the members drive a Honda! So Security, if they're on the ball, is supposed to redirect the car to one of our locations where the public's always welcome. And they're supposed to do it before anyone notices."

Embry has difficulty phrasing a question.

"Enjoy your shake!" says Sue brightly.

"Wait! I don't get it."

Sue frowns. "I have orders up. Get Mister Ziegler to explain."

"I'm not sure we have that kind of relationship," says Embry.

Sue looks at her wristwatch. "I have a break coming in about a half hour. I can't talk until then."

"What's your last name?"

"Why do you want to know?"

Usually a fumbler with women, Embry is amazed to hear himself deliver a fairly smooth response. "Because I mean to get your phone number, and if I lose it I want to be able to find you again."

She gives him a so-it's-like-that-is-it kind of look. "Budgen," she says, and smiles.

Sue Budgen.

Such a nudge soft, nipple-y name.

There's a good bit that Embry doesn't comprehend, like what's up with the door, the vanishing car, and his unaccustomed social fluency, but he assumes the drugs are responsible and shunts these issues aside in favor of a mental dalliance with Sue that begins on the couch of his West Hollywood apartment, progresses through marriage, kids, a long decline into old age, followed by a spectacular afterlife during which, eternally young, they wander a vast country of parklands, gentle, exotic animals, and Cecil B. DeMille sunsets, engaging in threeways with a variety of lovely, pneumatic, large-eyed, uniquely attractive aliens of several different species, deciding by means of these contacts in which form they will be reborn.

•⊩————⊪•

AFTER HIS first bite of lunch Embry bumps Key Lime pie down a notch on his list of Favorite Foods and slots Dreamburgers into the runner-up position behind his mamma's spoonbread, a ranking the buttery southern soufflé has maintained primarily due to nostalgia. A Dreamburger is the Ur-hamburger, the grilled meat patty from which all others derive their mana, and he honors it by devouring every crumb of meat and crisp onion and lightly toasted bun in six or seven bites. Pausing to catch his breath before beginning his second Dreamburger, he spies fifteen or twenty raspberry-skinned demons not much bigger than ants, with tiny horns and spear-point tails, scrambling across the surface of Ziegler's Belgian waffle, jumping down into one or another of the grid of potholes indenting its surface, many of them filled with maple syrup, these forming virtual tar pits in which some of the demons have become trapped. Embry concocts a fictional history for them, documenting their escape from Hell in order to live more carefree existences, for they are a relatively playful sub-species, kinder than most...and then Ziegler's fork slices down, halving two of the playful imps. Raspberry ichor mixes with the maple syrup as he lifts the fork to his mouth, carrying into the darkness a pair of still-kicking legs and an upper torso and head that shakes a teensy fist at Ziegler, as if threatening to go down hard into that sinner's stomach.

Freshly paranoid, fearing an infestation, Embry peeks under his bun and catches sight of a Lilliputian raspberry-colored foot withdrawing beneath a lettuce leaf; to pursue it further, he would have to disassemble the burger, an act verging on desecration, and might have to forego eating it. Perhaps demons are what give Dreamburgers their special savor, or perhaps he's seeing things. Forcing himself to think of something other than raspberry blood, he munches away, washing each bite down with a swallow of milkshake that glides across his tongue like a swath of chocolate silk. Once done, he lets out a delicate burp, pats his mouth clean with a napkin and finds Ziegler grinning at him.

"How about some pie?" Ziegler asks. "They do a great coconut cream. Or you want to wait on dessert and chat about the movie a little?"

"Yeah, let's chat."

"Okey-dokey." Ziegler's grin widens to Cheshire cat proportions and his face acquires a roundness it does not ordinarily possess. "What made *Dragonslayer* unique?"

"The dragon?"

"We have a winner!" Ziegler winks broadly. "The dragon couldn't talk. It wasn't three hundred feet tall, it wasn't a magic dragon or a cuddly dragon. It was a big dirty lizard that lived in a cave littered with turds and ate the shit out of some virgins. How did Ray tell you he wanted you to handle it?"

"He said to make it nasty."

"Ray's a master of understatement," Ziegler says. "This has to be the nastiest fucking dragon ever. This dragon craps half-digested body parts. It licks the virgins up and fucking down before it bites off their tits. It smells like a century of beer farts. If it were a human being, it'd be a child molester with boils and psoriasis."

"What I was thinking," Embry says. "Have you seen *The Host*?"

Ziegler returns a blank stare.

"It's a film by Bong Joon-Ho," Embry goes on. "The Korean director? His monster's an amphibious creature the size of a bread truck and what's so cool is he manages to give it a personality..."

"This is a movie," says Ziegler sternly. "Not a *film*."

"Okay, but..."

"It's not going to be directed by some Korean pussy. We're talking to bankable guys."

"I know, but the way Bong Joon-Ho..."

"The guy's named Bong? What's his brother's name? Hash pipe? He's got a sister named Syringe?"

"Let me finish, okay? What's so great about *The Host* is how the monster's personality is developed. If we can anthropomorphize the dragon to an extent, give it some human characteristics, it'll be more horrible."

"I don't care."

"No, really. If you..."

"No, really. I don't care." Ziegler tips his head to the side, as if seeing Embry in a new light. "Ray said you were right for the picture, but here you go getting all art house on me. I'm starting to wonder if I can trust him on this."

Embry remains silent—silence is the only safe course at this juncture and has the added virtue of conveying the impression that he refuses to grovel, which (though far from the actual case) is not a bad impression to convey.

If Ziegler buys it, that is, and it's almost a guarantee that he does not.

Ziegler orders a slice of pie for himself, none for Embry, thus signaling his displeasure, and Embry turns to the window, trying to think best how to resurrect the conversation. Dark clouds with silvery edges have surged in off the Pacific and a few drops of rain show on the glass. He tracks the approach of another car, a Rolls Royce, a sleek, gray land-whale that makes it all the way to the parking lot. A short stocky white-haired man with thick black-rimmed glasses and beetling black eyebrows, instantly recognizable to Embry, climbs out of the Rolls and walks briskly to the door. Once inside, he makes a beeline for their booth and says peremptorily, "Mars!"

"Hey, how's it going, Marty?" says Ziegler.

Marty jerks a thumb at Embry. "Who's this?"

Embry extends a hand and says, "It's an honor to meet you, Mister..."

"What's on your mind?" Ziegler asks.

Marty glares at Embry; his eyebrows work up and down, bunching together like CGI caterpillars. Embry is amazed by how greatly he resembles a corpselike version of Mr. Potato Head.

"Want to talk about the fucking Japanese picture," he says gruffly to Ziegler.

"Let's meet for drinks, okay? Say around seven?" Ziegler nods at Embry. "I'm in the middle of something."

"Flying to New York this afternoon."

Ziegler's expression is pained. "Jeez, Marty. Can't we do this on the phone? I'm teaching here."

Marty's eyebrows do their comic dance. He begins speaking to Ziegler in what Embry at first mistakes for a foreign tongue, but quickly realizes must be the secret Hollywood language he's heard about...only now he's been exposed to it, he understands it isn't a true language. Marty's-and-Ziegler's lips shape words in English, but it's as if the transmission has been jammed and all Embry hears is uninflected gibberish composed of a single word repeated over and over.

"Yattica yattica yattica yattica," Marty says.

"Yattica?"

"Yattica yattica. Yattica yattica yattica yattica yattica."

"Okay, fine," says Ziegler, switching back to normal speech. "Grab a table. I'll be right over." Once Marty's out of earshot, he says, "Are you nuts? Marty hates being recognized by people he doesn't know. He's paranoid as a shithouse rat! It's gotten worse since he won the Oscar. He hires people to impersonate him so he can sneak in places without being noticed. And don't you fucking say, 'How could I have known?' All you got to do is look at the guy, you can see he's a freak." He nails Embry with a stern gaze. "Don't do anything more to embarrass me."

⋅⊩———⊪⋅

THE CLOUDS scudding over the diner have darkened, but there will likely be no more than scattered raindrops—it's a weather that frequently occurs in LA and environs, this broken promise of a downpour, as if God's decided at the last minute not to waste the water, inspiring in Embry apocalyptic visions of a desert place that he once thought stunningly original, but now recognizes are essentially outtakes from the last *Resident Evil* sequel.

"If you still want to talk, go out back through the kitchen," says Sue, popping up beside the booth. "I'll meet you there in a minute."

Embry can't remember why he wanted to talk and when he does remember he wonders why he bothers. During his years in Hollywood every door he's opened has admitted to a startling new depth that, once he has adapted to it, he never re-encounters. Explanations of local mores and situational road maps are therefore irrelevant. Furthermore, he's convinced that this thing with Sue will lead nowhere—even if it doesn't, he believes he'll disappoint her or she him; but talking to her offers a brighter prospect than remaining in the booth, ducking the who's-that-knob stares of the rich and famous.

The cook, a monstrously squat entity, has a mottled neck that expands and contracts like a bullfrog's as Embry passes behind him, squeezing between a refrigerator and butt cheeks the approximate size of a triceratops'. As Embry cracks the door, the cook makes a low gurgling noise that may be an attempt to communicate, but Embry ignores it, not wishing to waste time in deciphering what may be another secret language, and steps out into the open, under a sky appreciably stormier than it was scant moments before. Ozone tickles his nasal membranes. The delicate rumblings of distant thunder drown out ambient noise from the freeway. Green lightnings flicker and slabs of cloud (gone a chocolate-y brownish black redolent of topsoil found in the Altiplano region of Guatemala) are breaking up and churning in the manner of an ugly ice floe, circling a patch of caliginous blackness and forming into a funnel, a slow inverted tornado. Embry studies the heavens and recalls an astrologer, a college pal named Ron, who advised him that Uranus, planet of drugs, was all over his chart, and that he would benefit from continued substance abuse. Though Ron's every other prediction about his future has proved unreliable, Embry relies on this particular counsel to keep him safe from a myriad of potentially dangerous chemical cocktails, much as one relies on a charm. He thinks his affinity for drugs must be serving him well, because it's clear now, if it was not before, that he is massively fucked-up, possibly in need of some Valium. In addition to the hallucinatory sky, the land behind the diner in no way resembles the post-industrial wasteland through which he passed prior to arriving at the Mouth of Hell. Instead, the scene is pure English pastoral, meadows and hedgerows stretching to the horizon, with here and there a fragment of oak forest, a scatter of placid black-and-white cows munching on lush verdure, unmindful of the maelstrom overhead—the whole thing puts him in mind of a Pink Floyd album cover, perhaps a lost recording bridging the gap between the clumsiness of *Atom Heart Mother* and the nascent genius of *Meddle*.

Dream Burgers at the Mouth of Hell   LUCIUS SHEPARD

Embry's speculations about the Brit prog band vis-à-vis their alternative development during the post-Syd Barrett years are cut short by Sue's emergence from the diner. She drops wearily into a lawn chair, one of four lined up against the rear wall, and lights a cigarette—he also sits, after turning an adjoining chair so he won't have to peer at her sideways. She's bustier than he recalls, with slightly darker hair, altogether a marginally coarser item than the Sue of his memory; but given his condition he feels lucky that she doesn't manifest eyes that shine like bad radiation and that tiny green witches aren't crawling in and out of her nostrils. She purses her lips and blows a double smoke ring that dissipates on the breeze.

"This place sucks ass," she says.

Neither this comment nor her expertise in the smoking arts synchs with the All American Child-Woman image she earlier presented, but Embry understands the need for a public face, especially for those who labor in the food-service industry.

"I'm going to ask for a transfer," she says after another puff. "Maybe to one of the San Luis Obispo shops. You wouldn't mind living there, huh? You could commute."

She appears to have gone a tad farther with the fantasy of their possible mutuality than he, something he finds both encouraging and disturbing.

"It's a franchise?" he asks. "There's a Mouth of Hell in San Luis Obispo?"

"Must be a few thousand of 'em."

"There can't be that many!"

"Why not?" She shoots him a perplexed look. "There's at least that many San Luises."

Confused, Embry isn't sure he heard her correctly. "So are they all alike…like MacDonalds?"

"Inside they're different, you know, according to region. The Honolulu shops have Tiki bars. The doors are the same, of course, and they all lead to the same place."

"Unh." Embry chews this over a time or two, trying to make sense of the bits and pieces he's learned. "Wait! What do you mean?"

Sue ignores the question. "You'd think these bastards would have evolved beyond the ass-grabbing stage." She clutches his forearm. "You won't treat me that way, will you? I mean, I want you to grab my ass from time to time, but not while you're snickering with your buddies."

A shadow overhead distracts Embry. He glances up, hoping to isolate the source, but it's difficult to make out a specific shape against the tumult of the sky—the moiling clouds produce such a variety of form, it's possible to see anything one wants.

"I'm sorry. I know you're not like that." Sue leans forward and gives him a kiss of the sort he associates with long intimacy, brisk yet with a little tongue. "It's just I get so worn down by those jerks, I start thinking you're all like that." She stands, smoothes down her uniform over her hips. "Is there something more you wanted to ask me, or can it wait until after work? I need to get back."

Dream Burgers at the Mouth of Hell LUCIUS SHEPARD

Embry tries to marshal his verbal skills, to pick the perfect interrogative from among the many fragmentary considerations circulating through his brain, but can't come up with anything apart from dumb relationship questions. Who are you? Are we dating? How can this be? Etc.

"Oh, look!"

Sue does a little bounce on her toes and points off into the fields, seemingly made giddy by the sight of a dragon alighting in the midst of the Pink Floyd-esque Holsteins, sending them into a panicked trot away from the source of danger. The dragon ignores them, emits a liquid coughing noise and barfs up a copious quantity of translucent slime. It's a biggish lizard, having the mass of approximately five cows, and impressively ugly, with skin the texture of cooked bacon, brown with a faint greenish sheen, as if it's been left out too long, and wings that, when folded, enclose its sides in a shawl of what appears to be masticated beef jerky. The head calls to mind that of a royal mastiff, protruding from the fancy ruff collar of its sagittal crest. It scoots about in apparent confusion, dragging its butt across the grass, reminding Embry of how Robin, his father's Springer spaniel, acted when he had worms, and the way it lumbers forward when it spots its quarry, unable at first to gather its legs beneath itself, like a coltish pup on a linoleum floor...For all its menace and grossness there is a distinct and somewhat goofy dog-like aspect to the beast. Embry is so absorbed in studying it that only belatedly does he recognize that he and Sue are the dragon's quarry.

"Eep," he says, staggering up from the chair.

"The gate's shut, dummy!" Sue gives his arm a playful punch. "It must be six months since I've seen a dragon. Isn't it amazing?"

Embry would agree that it's amazing, but sees no gate. He attempts another warning and succeeds in producing an attenuated version of his previous noise: "Ee-eee-eep!"

"You're such a silly!" Sue dances away from the diner, turns to face Embry, hikes up her skirt and bends over, flashing the dragon.

Galumphing toward her, its breath chuffing, bringing with it a smell like a swamp mingling with an open sewer, the dragon covers the intervening distance in a trice and, tipping its head to the side, an oddly delicate maneuver for such a monstrosity, takes a bite, chomping her lower half into a bloody mulch. Her head-and-torso fall to the ground, followed by a single leg. It's unbelievable, and Embry tries hard not to believe it, but the spray of warm arterial blood that has drenched him is eminently believable. He stands trembling, transfixed by the image of Sue's empty, open-eyed face and severed torso lying a few feet away, leaking intestines and gore. The dragon pokes its snout into the blood track extending from her torso and snorts, or maybe it's a sneeze, and snaps the tidbit up, tosses back its head, and lets it slide headfirst down its gullet. His resources drained, knowing that he's about to die, Embry stumbles backward and fetches up against the side of the diner. The dragon gives another snort, farts hugely, and noses Sue's leg, nudging it along through the grass as if not certain it wants to consume this particular delicacy, but finally snaps it up and once again throws back its head. The shape of the leg becomes visible, pressed against the interior of its throat. Gargling, grating noises, and the dragon shakes its head wildly. Its wings open partway. Embry understands it's choking. The leg is stuck in its maw. He slumps down against the rear steps, watching the dragon trying to back away from its pain, pawing at its throat, yellowish snot oozing from its nostrils, thick ropes of drool bridging between the fangs. The dragon's head sinks lower; its struggles grow less forceful. Embry regains the power to hate and begins to enjoy the beast's suffering, to relish each futile display, each groan and whimper. With a mighty effort, perhaps its last, the dragon lifts its head and vents a feeble scream that, of a sudden, evolves into a great retching noise—it vomits a gusher of slime and blood and soft pulpy things, a pinkish spew that splatters against the rear wall of the diner...and against Embry. Then it roars, a potent sound of triumph that, along with the apprehension of what those soft pulpy things must be, causes Embry's lights to dim. Before he passes out, the dragon's dopey canine-face-with-fangs swells in his vision, its jaws agape; as it pushes near, however, coruscant white sparks surround its snout and it jerks back its head...

•‖———‖•

WHEN EMBRY wakes he's sitting in the booth he shared with Ziegler, who's off at another booth, doing something to somebody. He's a little agitated, but his heart is no longer racing, his clothes appear to have been replaced with pricey replicas (the sleeve of his jacket feels like raw silk) and there's no trace anywhere of blood, slime or pulpy tissue. This persuades him that everything he witnessed was the product of hallucination, and that he is hallucinating still, though not to such extremes as before. He's thankful, yet remains on edge, a little uncertain of reality.

"So." Ziegler sits opposite him. "Bet you can write that dragon picture now." He plucks a toothpick from the dispenser and picks at something trapped between his teeth, perhaps a raspberry-skinned fragment. "Too bad about the babe, but that's the price of art, right?"

Embry blinks rapidly.

"Shake it off, dude!" Ziegler says. "You look like somebody stole your cookie."

"The dragon…what it did to Sue? It was real?"

"This is Hollywood." Ziegler chuckles. "Are fake tits real? Answer: Yeah…when a couple of big ones are massaging your dick."

Embry can't speak.

"You're going to breeze past this," says Ziegler. "You may hate me for a few, but a year from now you'll bless my name."

He says more, but Embry has stopped listening and is staring at Sue, who comes bopping along the aisle. When she notices him, her face lights up.

"I'm sorry! I got caught in a rush and couldn't get away." She fishes a slip of paper from her breast pocket and presses it into his palm. "You still want to talk, maybe you could give me a call?"

Flabbergasted, Embry manages an acknowledgment. He has no doubt that this is the original Sue, svelte of limb and large of tooth, not the bustier, coarser model who was dragon-munched out back; he's alarmed by how much of a difference this makes as regards his feelings about the episode. Sue briefly hovers beside the booth, flirting, then goes off. Embry asks Ziegler what the fuck is happening.

"When you get your membership packet, they give you a manual that'll explain things. It's yea thick." You could slip a Dreamburger between Ziegler's forefinger and thumb. "A bunch of gearhead shit—I can't ever get it straight. Now if you want to know about the multiple Sues, I can maybe shed some light."

Sue makes a brief return, setting a coffee drink in front of Embry, who eyes it suspiciously.

"Drink it," says Ziegler. "It's a pick-me-up."

Embry has a sip—it is, of course, delicious.

"First thing you need to know," says Ziegler. "Life is like a bowl of lamb stew."

Trying for sarcasm, Embry says, "Don't you mean it's like a box of chocolates?"

"Zemeckis brought his scriptwriter in for a meal before turning him loose on Gump. He very well may have gotten the idea here. But life is like a bowl of lamb stew. The simmering stew of what we see, the mirage heating on the hotplate of existence, the pieces of lamb and potatoes and carrots and celery and whatnot bobbing on the surface. With the slightest of upheavals, they can be dragged under the surface, into the suffocating brown muck of the real. The Mouths of Hell are what maintain things in a balance. They keep the pretty bits floating, looking fresh and succulent. They forestall the ultimate triumph of the muck. They sustain the illusion. You follow?"

"I guess."

"Yeah, I don't get it, either. Read the manual. And don't ask who's making this movie, because I don't have a clue. I suppose you have to take the name literally. The Mouth of Hell. But who's producing in Hell these days? The Illuminati? Secret Tibetan masters? All I know is, some big industry people are deeply involved." Ziegler rubs his hands together, getting back to business. "Now when you're inside a Mouth, you can access every part of the muck from the control room. If you use the right tool, you can reach in and grab a specific piece of celery or a pearl onion or a carrot chunk, because life is like…"

Ziegler makes a come-on gesture and Embry finishes his sentence: "A bowl of lamb stew."

"Exactly. So management grabbed you a second Sue. A juicy piece of lamb."

"We talking alternate universes or something?"

"Something. There's a lot of repetition. Anyway, this Sue, the one they grabbed, she's a pretty iffy article.

Convicted of matricide and then freed on a technicality. So don't go getting all maudlin."

Embry has a flash vision of the severed torso. "No one deserves to die like that."

"I'm not saying she did. Nor am I saying mistakes aren't made. But that's the way it's always been in LA. Chicks come looking for the big time and wind up on a coroner's table. Some are nice girls, some are sweater hogs. What do you fucking care? This Sue, your Sue, is still kicking. She wants you to call her and she didn't kill her mommy." Ziegler waggles a hand, trying to attract Sue's attention. "Check, please!"

•╫————╫•

WHAT'S TROUBLING Embry as he exits the diner is the ease with which he has moved past watching a woman torn apart, and though there are extenuating circumstances, not the least of which being that he isn't sure any of it actually happened, he nonetheless believes that a sense of unease is not a reaction commensurate with so traumatic an event. He's diverted from these concerns, however, on noticing the barren hills that ring the diner have evolved from smooth, brown dune-like slopes into sage-tufted, craggy elevations, their lower reaches populated by ranks of saguaro cactus, looking like an army of faceless green soldiers caught in the act of surrender. He assumes this to be a last production of the drugs he's ingested, but as they whizz along the freeway the hallucinations proliferate, ranging from minor disturbances in the air, trivial as heat haze, to a mass of writhing tentacles obscuring the roof of the Walt Disney Concert Hall; and he begins to wonder if this is what Ziegler meant when he said that on occasion someone "slips off their track." Embry's too paranoid to ask. Once Ziegler learns that he's off-track, he may kick him out onto the side of the freeway or, if he doesn't want to litter, will convey him to the lair of a giant worm whose digestive system leads to black hole destinations. Perhaps his inability to process the drugs signifies that he has failed a crucial test and so this self-absorbed mutant with dyed hair, caps, and delicate surgical scars is driving him to an execution terminal where defectives are funneled into disintegration machines. There are choices to be made and Embry is poorly equipped to make them, alternately gripped by fear and delirium. Should he seek a noble oblivion, grab the wheel and wrench it sideways, sending the Bugatti jolting across the safety island and into the path of an oncoming semi, thereby ridding the world of a notable excrescence and sparing it another hideous dragon picture? Or (if this is still an option) should he write the script and take his place among the regulars at the Mouth of Hell, accepting the inevitable loss of a soul in exchange for a lifetime of outstanding dental care? It's a tough call. Embry's teeth have long been a problem.

Ziegler asks if he would like to see what the Bugatti can do and Embry gets too busy pondering the sinister potentials of the question to frame a response, imagining scalpels and tubes emerging from the dash to plunge into his flesh; black butterflies with wings made of a metal denser than a dark star fluttering from the AC vents and covering him head-to-toe, compressing his body until it's the size of a homunculus, a tiny pale relic that will adorn Ziegler's trophy case.

They drive in silence a while and then, out of the blue, Ziegler says, "I was kidding about the cologne."

Embry doesn't get the reference and goes, as is his wont, "Huh?"

"The new car smell. It's because the car's new, not because I'm wearing cologne. That was all bullshit."

Trivial confession or crucial revelation, Embry can't divine which this is; but Ziegler's words seem to trigger a flushing away of past associations. Soon he's blank, almost empty of thought and feeling. A basic sense of self and scraps of memory are all that remain. He recalls being a member of the Karl Marx Society in college—though he never acquired the courage of his convictions, since his arrival in the capital of diseased celebrity and bawdy commerce he has come to recognize anew that the great man's welding of Hegelian dialectic to the materialism of Feuerbach is a model of economic virtue. Then that, too, is flushed away and he is left with pornographic imagery (Sue in several promising poses) and hallucinations (curiously jointed insects the size of Lear jets are spilling out of what appears to be a song lyric complete with cartoon-style sheet music notation in the sky above the US Bank Tower). This vacancy, he thinks, must be prelude to something and he looks to Ziegler, bug-eyed Martian, Mars to his buds, mentor to a promiscuity of hacks, in hopes that he will pronounce some magically glib homily that will fill him with a fresh spirit, permitting him to go forward.

"Yattica yattica," Ziegler says with stern assurance. "Yattica yattica yattica yattica."

Relieved, terrified, hopeful, uncertain, and most of all ashamed, Embry finally understands.

TESTAMENTS

JAY LAKE

*T*HE *Testament of the Six Sleeping Kings* is bound in ebon plates so dark that they drink all light that flows before them. Brilliance born in the fires of the sun, taking a thousand years to rise to the surface and eight minutes to leap across the stygian depths of space from the daystar to the humble Earth, only to be swallowed with the same finality as any rattling blade dropped upon a shuddering, aristocratic neck.

These are the hard truths: Some words were never meant to be read. Some thoughts cannot be undone. Some darknesses shall never be dispelled.

Some people will never believe these truths.

•╫———╫•

THE BOOK OF DREAMS

THE FIRST SLEEPING KING

IN A time before countries had borders, when birds filled the skies like raindrops in a storm, and the great migrations of the beasts had not yet been halted by walls and fences and fields, there lived a man named Linnel, youngest son to Ezar. In a hard land of withered olive trees, struggling cedars, salty ponds and miles of sere rocky hills, he was born to no great consequence, son of an ageing goatherd and the second of his father's three wives.

His first-mother, Aranu, had already forgotten herself and lay within her tent of hides moaning, except when she wandered smeared with shit and ashes to search for a baby who had died half a lifetime before Linnel's birth. His third-mother, Raha'el, had been a servant girl taken on more out of pity than need, then bound in marriage to stop the gossip about his father's undeniable concupiscence. His second-mother, who had carried Linnel into the world, was Aranu's much-younger cousin, Tobeth, who stood midway in years between her co-wives.

Thus Linnel had grown up beneath Ezar's hard hand—for goats are unforgiving, and their masters learn this from the animals themselves—burying Aranu when he was nine years of age and finding his way into Raha'el's bed when he was twelve.

All in all, an unremarkable childhood in that time and place before the morning of the world had been set by those who first chose to keep time.

Until the dream came.

It was the dawn of his fourteenth birthday. Raha'el had celebrated with Linnel the night before, suckling him to her breast and calling him her best child until Linnel's staff had hardened enough for him to be her biggest man instead. As always he took her in the manner of a boy so there would be no chance of get. After she'd wrung her pleasures from her son, Raha'el had sent him away, lest Ezar be forced to take notice of these nocturnal excursions. No one was fooled, but the niceties were kept.

Except that morning Linnel lay on a goathide amid a meadow of tiny night-blooming flowers. Already they shut their pale colors and delicate scents away against the first hot breeze of day trickling down from the stony hills to the east. A light descended from the sky in a stink of brimstone and old ash.

Linnel sat up, startled, all too conscious of Raha'el's passion still glistening on his thighs and amid the downy fuzz of his beard. A torch, thrown by an invader? He was unprepared for anything except a wash in the goats' pond. Cursing, he realized even his sling was in his tent, too far to reach now.

But a torch would have fallen with the speed of any stone, and this light drifted like a wind-born seed.

—*Linnel*, said a voice out of the very air itself.

"Aranu?" It was all he could think, that his first-mother had found her way out from beneath the stones of her grave in search of her lost infant.

—*Malakh.*

Linnel realized he heard a name. It meant 'messenger' in the tongue of a people who sometimes traded with Ezar for goats, but this being of light was clearly not one of the She'm. Uncertain if this was an ancestor or a spirit of the air or some creature whose nature had never been communicated to him, the boy dropped on one knee.

"I serve."

—Fire.

With that word, Malakh told Linnel a story, a tale which raged inside his head, of the birth of the world from boiling rocks hotter than even the heart of a smith's fire, of rains which quenched the land until storms of steam and vapor finally ceased, of the intention which made plants and trees, then birds and beasts, and finally rising like a pomegranate tree from spilled seeds, people themselves, fire's great-great-grandchildren.

"I know," Linnel said, and wondered if he dared address this being more directly.

—Honor.

With that word, he knew what must come next. Such a power in the world deserved respect, fear even, and substance; not the soiled thrustings and small betrayals of a family forever encamped on the hillsides of this land.

"I obey."

Opening his eyes, Linnel strode back into their camp and took up his father's thornwood staff where it lay propped outside Ezar's tent. He used the ageing tool as a weapon to restore honor to himself and the Messenger of the fire. He almost turned away from his course when he saw Raha'el's blood fresh upon her heaving breasts as she screamed her last, but her dying curse propelled Linnel to his father's tent with his resolve renewed.

"The path must be made ready that people will know who stands above us," he told the three fresh graves, hasty cairns assembled before a puzzled audience of wary goats. "We must know our sins before we can repent them."

Eating of a withered apple, Linnel strode away from his bleating charges towards the more fertile lands lower down and coastwise, already framing the words of his tale that people might properly understand their import.

His steps slowed for a moment when he began to wonder if the being of light had been a dream or a true sending, but the sacrifice was made. He was committed. Dream or no dream, this was his path.

●II————II●

THE ANGEL'S pen nib was wrought of the stuff of stars, a metal so dense and fierce that it could almost fold space around itself. The ink it used was distilled from the blood of a dozen dozen saints—what use sinners, when they are as common as sand at the seashore, and thus of no import at all? The parchment was stripped from the hide of a broken god, stretched and scraped on frames of living bone.

●II————II●

THE SECOND SLEEPING KING

MASSAH OFTEN walked in dreams. He had learned to do this long before he realized it was any trick at all. Even as the smallest child there had been the steps taken on chubby, uncertain feet amid the veiled ladies of the royal court; and there had been the steps that unfolded before his inner eye, sleepwalking on clouds and the backs of crocodiles and the memories of the day.

The mystery and miracle had arrived for Massah when he finally understood that almost no one around him did this thing. Pten, the withered old priest who always smelled of grave dust and bird droppings, certainly had the secret. They'd even met, in the other lands. There, Pten was a broad-chested young man with skin the color of old tea. Much more handsome than the pasty, hollow youth the priest had doubtless once been.

Pten always frowned at Massah, knowing him for a dreamwalker, but had not then sorted out who he was in the waking world. Massah, on the other hand, *knew* who it was he met in dreams. Always, and without fail.

So when he met the Angel of Death come for the woman who had raised Massah as though he were her own son, he knew enough not to try to bar the other's path. At the same time, Massah could not help but bid the stranger tarry a while, his secret hope to grant his mother a few more moments of life's breath.

"I know your errand," he told the angel.

The other looked at him with empty eyes. Like all the messengers of God, it was as perfect as a marble statue, slick-pale and unblemished, but its gaze was just as blank. The angel wore no armor except that of his studied magnificence, clad only in stone-hard skin and the regard of a distant deity. Even the sword of legend was absent.

—*All men know my errand, at least at the end of their days.* The angel's voice was as devoid of passion as its expression.

"All men are born to die," Massah replied. He was ever polite. Impolite people did not long remain behind the shaded walls and rambling bowers of the royal court. "Only a fool pretends otherwise."

—*Why does this fool pretend to converse with me, then?*

"I bargain for nothing but a few moments of your time. In payment I offer my own wit. Among some circles I am accounted a more than passing conversationalist."

—*She will not live a heartbeat longer.* A tinge of pity might have stained its voice.

Massah was ashamed then, and even afraid. "It was never my intention to waste your time, lord angel."

—*All of time is the lord God's. None will ever be wasted.*

The angel touched the side of Massah's head with a cold finger heavier than any stone.

—*Go back to your court and look beyond its walls, if you would see the price of life and the value of death.*

When Massah awoke he was forced to swallow his screams. He stumbled to the basin to banish the taste of embalming herbs from his mouth. In his reflection upon the water, Massah saw that his dark, curly hair had become white and brittle and straight where the angel had touched him. All thoughts of his mother fled him in the face of the strangeness of that gift from the angel of death.

He rose in time from his ablutions and subsequent meditations to don a heavier pair of sandals and a rough-spun robe, and pass outside the royal court through the gate called Envy, and into the bustling streets and marketplaces beyond.

There in the city of kings he found a world he'd always known of, but never considered with sufficient care. The people of his birth labored under great loads of clay and straw, sweating more than the donkeys of the merchants. Even the poorest of the kingdom were free to spit upon the slaves. Many did so, simply to find a moment when they could call their own lot better than another's.

Massah had been raised among the scent of lemons and the coolth of fountains. Now, his sandals slapping the dusty clay and worn cobbles of the streets, he realized that he had always been only a pet to the princesses and concubines who had dressed him in versions of princely raiment and taught him to twist his tongue in honeyed speech much as the smoothest courtiers did.

A joke.

A monkey, trained to ape his betters for the amusement of the women of the royal court.

Why had he never seen this in all his dreamwalking?

Because he'd been ashamed of the poor, starveling dreams of slaves.

He began to run, the smack of his sandals slapping against the stones of the city that had always sheltered him. Massah sprinted past obelisks and the blank faces of temples and fly-clouded ossuaries and clay pits where his countrymen worked naked in the rending heat. He raced as if he could outrun the very touch of the angel gone past.

On his return to the royal court, a death was being cried.

Of course.

His mother.

The priests demanded to know where Massah had been. Old Pten nodded with a dark leer. Long conversations were held in small, hot rooms. A senior prince stormed in, and Massah thought he might die then on a bronze blade, but the prince departed again as temple gongs began to echo across the palaces of the royal court.

In time, he was left alone with his thoughts. Massah understood what the angel of death had shown him. Every people had their time under the brassy gaze of heaven. He could forestall the doom of none. But he could change the price of life.

He dreamed again, of rivers of blood and rains of frogs and the stilled heartbeats of every firstborn son in the city. Walking in dreams, Massah made it so in the hot lands of the waking world, until the streets themselves cried as never he had for his mother's death.

THE ANGEL wrote in a language possessing only one word, though that word was of infinite length. All the syllables of creation echoed in the letters it scratched across the weeping pages. They did not remain static as ink on vellum might, but writhed in their own private torments, recalling the souls rendered to make them so.

•╫────────╫•

THE THIRD SLEEPING KING

THE BRIDGEBUILDER was a man out of his place. He'd been raised by Attic tutors among marbled halls on a hilltop overlooking a glass-green sea. He'd learned the classics, he'd studied rhetorics and logic and law and the histories of empire. He'd answered questions and stood for examinations and dutifully learned the arts of sword, shield, spear and horse. In short, the Bridgebuilder had been forged to be the sort of man needed in every corner of the empire.

Then the Senate had sent him to a land he'd never meant to visit, to rule over a people with no sense of their needs—only a burning, passionate purpose transcending all reason.

Out of place, even out of time he sometimes thought. Certainly the Bridgebuilder lived in a palace, but it was so unlike the wind-whispered halls of his youth. His servants were for the most part sullen would-be poisoners kept in line only by the ever-present guards. The land itself rejected the empire, with short harvests and failing fisheries and blights on the olive groves and date palms, so even the most hard-hearted tax gatherer came back with chests half empty.

People who have nothing can pay nothing. It was a lesson these fools had taken to heart, until the Bridgebuilder began to wonder if they had fouled their own wells out of sheer, raw spite.

His only relief came in the light wine that was made up in the hills and shipped down to the lowlands in resinous casks. The flavor reminded him of the piney ferments the servants of his youth drank, which was fine with the Bridgebuilder. He had no pretensions to be anything other than a hopeless colonial, unworthy of the exacting standards of the Eternal City whose empire he served. He would never sit in the Senate, or aspire to a voice at the emperor's ear.

He just wished mightily that he was anywhere but this miserable post.

Even the nights were hot through most of the seasons. The Bridgebuilder would take his resinous wine and two or three of the serving girls and retire to his apartments on the roof of the palace. There he would command them to bathe him with sponges soaked in watered vinegar. After that he would command them to bathe one another. There was always room among his silks for an extra girl, and as the people of this place hated his virtues as much as they hated his vices, the Bridgebuilder indulged himself regardless.

One girl in particular he had favored for a handful of seasons—Saleh. She was willing to lie with him in whatever manner pleased him. On nights when he was too far gone in wine to know his own mind, she would lie with him in whatever manner pleased her. And she was never jealous of any favor he showed to other girls. Best of all, she would hold him when the weeping came upon him, and whisper him to sleep with counsels which felt wise in the watches of the night, whatever his morning wit might later make of them.

So it was that Saleh came to be his confidante in matters of state. Often as not, he wept for sheer frustration, once the wine had done its work. They curled together amid billowing curtains and the salt smell of the nearby ocean as she listened, and spoke, and listened.

"Is that priestly council your master?" she asked him one time during a particularly difficult bout of religious revivalism among the occupied peoples.

The Bridgebuilder waved off the suggestion. "No, no, I serve only the demands of empire. My orders come by courier aboard fast galleys, not from a bushel of black-robed schemers on their temple steps."

"Of course," Saleh said. She kissed his ears, nibbling on the edges as he loved so much. "So their words are as the barking of dogs to you, yes?"

"Yes," he said, sighing. "I mean, no. No. I cannot simply order them to act. I do not have soldiers enough to dictate from every street corner."

"So you are beholden to their goodwill." Something glinted in her voice, an edge he had not often heard—or noticed—before.

"Never." Pride stirred within him, a sluggish beast long put to sleep by the sheer unreasonableness of this place.

"You are the lion of this land," Saleh told him. Her hand, oiled now, slipped down to once more seek proof of his manly worth. "Do not let them shave your mane."

Later, lost in restless sleep, the Bridgebuilder was visited by two men from out of time. One had the seeming of a savage, freshly descended from some blood-soaked mountaintop. The other was a man of courtly bearing, wrapped in the grave-pale linens of Egypt long past.

—*You deserve your name,* the savage said.

—*And the joy of your position,* added his companion.

They spoke in a sort of chorus:

—*Do not judge for the rabble. That is no better than choosing between two rotten fruits. When you are done, you still have only rotten fruit to show for your labors.*

"Who are you?" he asked.

—*Sleeping kings of old.*

Not my kings, the Bridgebuilder thought, but he had too much respect for the power of the dream to speak thusly.

Soon after he refused to hear a case. A man was set to die for some pointless heresy, when the Bridgebuilder could have freed him. "The choice of rotten fruits does not appeal to me," he haughtily told the delegation of local priests. Saleh had smiled at him from the shadows, but he never saw her again.

In time, the Bridgebuilder realized that she, too, had been part of the dream; prophecy gone wrong without him ever knowing how to set it to rights.

•⊞———⊞•

THE ANGEL recorded as faithfully as only one of its kind could do. Mindless in their devotion, they were not made to question. That was the province of men and women, those failed echoes of the creator. Words twisted as much as they ever had, crossing the bridge of meaning between intent and actuality. Still, the page held them.

•⊞———⊞•

THE FOURTH SLEEPING KING

THE MAID buckled her armor. She was so very tired. The messenger angels did not come so much any more. It had all been so clear in the years before she'd picked up a sword. Voices in the hayloft, visions of light by night. God spoke through His servants and she listened.

She was the maid. This was the way of things.

Now she was accounted an enemy even by the very people she'd saved. The invaders from across the water, of course, said terrible things of her. The maid knew to expect that. Scullery girls argued in the same fashion. In a way, it was an honor to have her name on the lips of enemy nobles. She was the only woman they did not ignore.

But her own countrymen had turned away from her as well. Their hate bloomed the red-gold colors of mounting flames as surely as the leaves turned away from summer when autumn stole across the forests. This she could not understand. Had she not pressed the fight at Orléans and Jargeau? Had she not saved the very life of the Duke of Alençon?

There was the truth, of course. To be saved by a woman was more disgraceful than to have been defeated by a man. Their ears were open to the charges whispered from across the water, spread in those places where the armies met and mingled on saints' days, in whore's beds, at market towns, around council tables.

God had not forsaken her, but her own people had.

Still, she wore these good greaves and chain over a surcoat. Still, she had the helmet dented by a dozen arrows, each turned away in the last moment by an angel's hand, even while those closest to her fell. Still, she had this sword. The ultimate blasphemy, far beyond the worried mutterings of the priests—that a woman should take up the most male of weapons and prove herself able to cut and thrust her way into the body of the enemy soldiers and their army alike.

With that thought, she sat to oil and whet her blade. This had not been in the morning's plan. Mist rose off the fields outside her tent, the smell of horses and campfires, the little sounds of an army waking to a battle day. Even the sound of footsteps echoing on stone was not enough to deter her from her task, though they reminded her that the rest of this was memory, or dream.

Stroke the blade. Metal gleamed in the oil, a false brilliance which dried all too soon, but for a while made this a sword of heaven. The whicking sound of the whetstone against the edge. The heft of the pommel, more familiar to her now than the hands of any of the lovers she'd never taken in her years among men. The rotten straw reek of the cell where she knew she slept, even as the dream-sword found its edge.

—*There is no more to be done.*

She stiffened, the sword falling away from her hand even though there was no clangor of the blade striking the ground. The stuff of dreams, as real as it had been. This was the first time the Lord's host had spoken to her in... how long? "I am content," the maid lied.

—*No one is content facing their end.*

"The end of my life on earth is but the beginning of my place in heaven," she replied piously. Though in truth, she'd long doubted that as well. Too many of the men she'd killed were simply men. Not demons or devils, but ordinary persons with wives and children who ate too much and farted and slept uneasily and cursed their serjeants and prayed upon their knees to the same God she did.

Could she truly climb to heaven on a stairway made of the corpses of men who'd died with the Lord's name upon their lips?

—*Yes.* Of course the angel could hear her thoughts.

With that the maid once more knew this for a dream. The messenger spoke in the words of the enemy, which were not so different from her own Frankish speech, but always before they had whispered to her in the writhing tongue of angels, which is far more like the stirring of snakes in some nest, or the rising of a locust horde, than any simple words from the mouth of a woman or man.

Had the conversations always been dreams?

—*Yes,* the angel said again.—*But what does it matter? The world is but a dream of God. You will be a king in the history of this dream.*

"A king in death?" she asked aloud. "Surely a queen."

—*No simpering queen drew on armor and sword,* the angel told her reproachfully.

Queens do not simper, the maid thought, and turned her face away until she tasted straw in her mouth and awoke to a bright morning with the memory of a sword's heaviness on her lap. The gaze of the priest before her smoldered, and the maid knew she, too, would soon smolder.

THE ANGEL paused in its labors. Its kind *were* Divine intent, in the most literal sense, and so the purposes of the Tetragrammaton were never a mystery. Still, the words spreading from its pen introduced an unheralded glimmer of doubt.

Doubt was heresy, doubt was the casting out, a star fallen from the crystal heavens to the deepest lake of ice far beneath the middle world of God's creation. Shrugging off the unaccustomed sense, the angel resumed its toils.

THE FIFTH SLEEPING KING

THE OLD man sat amid the willow trees and stared out across the Potomac. The waters of the river ran muddy, almost oily, seeming tired as they slipped home toward the sea. He'd been many things. The cicadas in the trees hummed the story of his life.

Planter.

Surveyor.

Soldier.

Politician.

General.

President.

"But never king," he told the approaching night. In truth, surveyor had always been his favorite.

—Of course you were a king.

The old man looked up at the voice, which had carried over the cycling buzz of the insects. An angel stood before him—of this he had no doubt, for all his lifetime of tepid faith. Not recognizing this creature as one of God's messengers would be like not recognizing the ocean as being made of water.

It stood before him, a composite of mist off the river and the singing of slaves and the smell of the smokehouse and a few swirling leaves caught up in the hem of its robe. The old man knew he was dreaming then, but knew also that this, alone among all the dreams of his lifetime, was more real than even his waking moments.

"I beg your pardon," he said. "I went to some trouble never to be crowned."

—Kingship is not a matter of a circlet upon the brow. There was something almost prim in the angel's tone.

A question stole unbidden from his mouth. "Is my time at hand?" He was immediately ashamed of the fear that had asked it.

—*I am not that messenger.* Kindliness guttered in the angel's eyes, warming coals for the cold hands of the old man's soul.

He resolved to ask no more questions. That revelation should choose to come to him in the sunset of his days was no more, or less, surprising than any of the other things which had overtaken the old man down the now-vanished years. "I thank you for the visit, at least. Most who come to see me want something. Asking, always asking."

—*I ask nothing of you that you do not ask of yourself.* The angel moved, drawing the wind with it as a cloak, so the waters of the Potomac stirred in a way that would have alarmed any waterman.

"I ask nothing of myself." *Children,* thought the old man. Issue of his loins. A swift ending to the fractured mess the politics of his young nation had already become. A brake for the pride of those who had succeeded him in office both high and low. "Though sometimes I ask much of the world," he admitted with the same ruthless self-honesty that had so often been a stumbling block in his life.

The angel bent before him. Kneeling? —*Here is the secret of your life,* it whispered in a voice of willow leaves and the whippoorwill. When it began to speak again, all the old man heard was the dank, close sound of darkness, and the fading of Martha's crying. He stared at his trembling hands and wondered how long she would mourn him.

•⊪————⊪•

THE PEN scratched on. Scribing, scrying, painting futures in the ink of the past, though all time was one from the vantage of the angel's copydesk. It had recovered its equilibrium. Angels were pendulums, marking the endless moments of the mind of God, messengers bridging the ineluctable gap between perfected intent and the imperfect matter of Creation.

It had never questioned why God, Who was all things everywhere, should require a book to record His doings, or the doings of His creation. It is not the nature of angels to question, only to answer. It is not the nature of angels to devise, only to record.

•⊪————⊪•

THE SIXTH SLEEPING KING

WHAT THE hell was the matter with people? No respect, that was it. His mother had been right. No one ever listened to him like they should.

The man who had been commander-in-chief poured himself another drink. He wasn't supposed to, had given it up years ago so far as anyone knew. The gap between what he said he did and what he actually did had ceased to matter so long ago that the ex-commander-in-chief rarely considered it any more. What he said, what he *believed*, was the truth. The messy details were just that: messy details. No one's business.

Disappointment, that was it. So many things which should have happened never did. Promises from Scripture and politics alike had been betrayed by niggling traitors. No one saw his goodness, his rectitude. Not even Laura, who'd always stood beside him, shrouding her thoughts in a smile.

He really ought to have married a girl like Mom. A man could rule the world with a woman like that at his side. Daddy had, damn him.

The ice in his glass clinked like the fall of coins. The outside sweated cold and heavy. He knew then he was dreaming, he really hadn't touched a drink in years. Not really. Not that counted. The ex-commander-in-chief simply didn't stand around mixing a highball.

He had people to do it for him.

Even in his dreams, a man had to laugh at himself.

A young fellow in a suit stepped close. Dark skinned, but not obviously any particular kind of colored. The ex-commander-in-chief didn't recognize the guy, though he wore the regulation gray suit and translucent earpiece. —*Sir.* The fellow's voice slipped through another layer of dreaming into a space of soaring naves and thundering sermons and the safe, blind glory of prayer.

"This is about the red heifer, isn't it?" Where had *that* come from? He wasn't supposed to talk about it. The glory would come, in his lifetime, he'd been promised. He *knew.*

—*Sir.* Something hung in the fellow's eyes, expectant as a launch code.

He felt his breathing grow shallow and hard. "Is it time?" The promise, it was coming to pass!

—*Sir.*

A familiar peevishness rose inside him, that his handlers had so long fought to banish. Too bad for them, he was the boss here. Always would be. Didn't matter how he got to the top, nope. He was here now and not climbing down. No sir. "What is it," the ex-commander-in-chief demanded. "Speak up!"

—*Sir.* The voice sounded haunted, as if coming from an empty hallway far away.

He tried to shake off his dream, to wake up gasping amid the sheets. He hated the feeling of being wrapped in self-doubt, and always shed it as quickly as he could. Mother said too much thinking was bad for a man. The ex-commander-in-chief had learned to trust his gut. Facts changed depending on who brought them to you. Feelings were the hard truths.

Right now he was feeling very worried indeed.

—*Sir.* A terrible fire blossomed behind the fellow's gaze. The ex-commander-in-chief threw his drink at the flames, but they only passed outward along the arcs of liquid and ice and shattered glass until his dream was consumed by fire and a great voice echoed from the heavens, asking him if this was truly what he intended.

Still, he did not doubt himself. Not him. Nope. No sir.

THE ANGEL finally set aside its pen. The book was done, or would be until it was opened again. Words were the oldest, greatest magic. God had spoken in the beginning, and He would someday unspeak the end, swallowing Creation down in a sweeping blur of undoing: oaks shrinking to acorns; cold cinders swelling first to red giants, then reduced to their starry births; old men climbing from graves to step backwards to life until they climb puling and mewing back to the salty delta from which each had first flowed.

As done, undone. As lived, unlived. Time, helical, alive, autophagic, endless as a circle, with as many corners as an egg.

All of this best stated in the language of dreams. Consciousness was too linear for even the angel itself to properly comprehend the sweeping swirl of God's Creation. How so for His poor creatures of clay and sweat and breath?

It smiled, preening a moment, feeling a rare sense of accomplishment before moving on to the next task: to bear the book away so it might someday be read.

●‖————‖●

THE SEVENTH KING

SHE IS just a girl. She doesn't know her parents, though there are people who live in her house and clothe her and feed her and call her by a name not her own. At night a favorite uncle crawls out of the wainscoting, thin as a shadow, heavy as a star, and whispers to her the dreams of sleeping kings long dead.

Someday she will be so famous that they will have to write down her dreams. When she grows into her power and announces her true name, darkness will settle like a cloak, bringing the nighttime of the soul to all those who have plunged her into darkness.

Which is to say, all of everyone.

For now, dreaming is enough. There is no higher truth.

REX NEMORENSIS

KAGE BAKER

I GOT some Everclear. You want to sit down, have a drink?

No reason to freak, man.

Yeah, it's a grave. Grave of an old dude. Old dudes die all the time. I'll tell you about it.

I lived with my old lady when I got out of the Army. We had a nice life for a while. Were you in Nam? No? I guess you're too young. You a serviceman? No, huh? No, I won't tell you about it. I've told enough people about the war.

I just had these bad dreams, wouldn't quit. I'd wake up thinking there were gooks hiding in the house and I couldn't go back to sleep until I got up and checked things out. And one time I woke up and thought I was in bed with a gook and I laid Darla's lip open. I was sorry and she was cool about it, told the emergency room lady she'd fallen out of bed, but all the same we both knew I was losing it.

And then I shot Peaches and Snowball. The cat was a mistake, anybody would have done that, he was on the roof in the night. The dog...she did some stupid dog thing, I don't even remember what, and I lost it. But I was standing there with the gun in my hand and then Darla's face when she came running in, you know...she really loved that dog. That was when we both knew I had to go.

She was still cool about it. We stayed friends.

I made a camp back in the hills and came down to the shelter in the mornings, to shower and eat and like that. They had me talking to a doctor at the clinic for a while but then something changed and I wasn't eligible anymore. Sometimes Darla would come meet me in the park and we'd have a couple of beers. Then her shift got changed and she had to work days, so I didn't see her so much. We just sort of drifted apart. No hard feelings.

Then one day I'm sitting in the park and Smokey from the shelter comes by and gives me a piece of paper with a message and a phone number. Darla wants me to call her.

I say, "What's up, babe?" and she's crying because the plant closed and she's got to move back to Fresno where her folks live. And she paid first and last on our place and so she has to clear out pretty fast. She's been going through the garage and all my stuff is still there and what do I want to do with it?

So I go over to the house and some of my stuff I want, like the guns and the knives and a couple of jackets, but the rest I tell her I don't give a flying fuck, she can hold a yard sale or something. She says, "Okay, but what about your mother's trunk?" Which I'd forgotten about. So we get it out and go through it.

I'm feeling pretty bad because there's, like, baby pictures and stuff, and my birth certificate and Mom's and Dad's death certificates, and their wedding pictures and other shit. And some really old pictures that are, I guess, Mom's family. Old squashed flowers and a busted rosary, and everything smells like musty perfume. Darla cries and says I can't throw it all out and I say, "What am I going to do with it?" because it'll just get all rained on and ruined at my camp.

So she says she'll keep some of it for me. So we go through it figuring out what we're going to burn and what she wants to hang on to. And we find this deed to some land. And a map.

Darla says, "I didn't know your family ever owned any land" and I tell her I didn't know either. The deed's in the name of my other grandpa, who died in World War One. Darla says my Dad must have known about it, but I'm not so sure; the envelope they're in is sealed like it hasn't been opened since the day they were put in there. And if Dad had known he had some land, we wouldn't have ended up in that stinking trailer park in San Bernardino. My other grandma killed herself when Dad was nine, so he never got the chance to ask her about stuff. But there was this title deed, all along, and it sure would have come in handy back then.

Darla gets all excited and opens a bottle of wine. We sit down and go over it real careful and it's a deed all right, showing my grandpa paid the sum of three hundred dollars for a lot in the town of Legrand in San Luis Obispo County. It's got the county clerk's seal and everything. Darla says, "Oh my God, look, it's even near the beach!"

We get out an Auto Club map and look it up, but there isn't any town of Legrand on the Auto Club map. You can see the little towns just north and east, like they are now, but a great big empty space where Legrand was on the old map, and some words about a Dunes Recreational Area. So, see, I tell her, it *was* too good to be true. And Darla feels so bad about it she lets me go upstairs with her, one last time.

But I can't sleep afterward. Not used to sleeping in a house anymore and I keep thinking I hear somebody coming up the stairs. I'm lying there in bed thinking about things, and I decide the deed is worth checking out anyway.

Next morning I go through all the papers to get my birth certificate, and my Dad's birth certificate and all, so I can prove I'm the rightful heir. Darla loans me twenty bucks and kisses me goodbye. I wish things had worked out. You know a chick's in love when she'll hang on to your mom's death certificate for you.

Took me most of a week to get here, hitching and walking. You know, you think: the beach! Wow! And then you get here and instead of hotels and restaurants and surfers, all there is to see is spinach fields stretching off to some empty-looking dunes, and it's all foggy and cold even though it's fucking July.

But land is land, you know? So I hitched a ride into San Luis Obispo and went to the county offices. I got the runaround there for a while until finally this old guy comes out and has a look at my deed and says "Ohhhh, yeah, we used to see these every so often," and he tells me the thing's basically worthless, because the town never got built and there's no roads leading there except one that goes out to the Offroad Vehicle Recreation area. He says now and then some clown like me finds an old deed in a trunk and gets all excited.

I ask him what happens if I decide to claim it anyway and he tells me that's no use. I can't build a house on it; the area's zoned as parkland now. I'm getting mad and I say, "What if I sue the Park Service, man? My grandpa paid hard cash for this deed."

He kind of lowers his voice and leans forward and tells me that sometimes the County will cut a deal with people and pay them back the original price, in exchange for signing over the deed so the Park Service has clear title. It's been seventy-two years, after all, so they don't even legally have to do that. And he says I don't want the damn land anyway, really, and he'll show me why.

He points on the back wall where there's this big black-and-white blown-up photo taken from an airplane. He holds up my map next to it and there's the spinach

THE BOOK OF DREAMS

fields and the coastline and a big white area which is just miles of sand dunes, except for some black and gray places at the edge. And what that is, he says, is "riparian wilderness". Which means swamp. Nothing there but willow trees and poison oak. He points back and forth from my map to the wall to show me where my lot is, and it's right in the swamp.

I think, "Shit", and I ask him who I talk to about seeing if I can sign over the deed for some money. He writes out an address and the hours they're open and I can see by the time I get there they'll be closed, and it's Friday afternoon. So I leave. The library's right across the street and I go in to use the can. While I'm in there I get to thinking that maybe I can sue the heirs of the land developer.

I go to the reference desk and ask about the company name on the deed. The lady gets me down books on local history. You know, first the Indians, then the Spanish, then us, blah blah, and it was all just part of some ranch until 1900, when this cult—Rosicrucians or Theosophists or something—came out from back east. They bought up the land and built a tuberculosis sanatorium for guys coming back from the Spanish American War. Those vets came back with tuberculosis, same as we came back from Nam with all the shit we caught.

And the next year they sold part of the land to the developer who laid out Legrand and sold lots. But then he couldn't get the Southern Pacific to build a station anywhere close to Legrand. Then, people started suing him when they got to the lots and saw they'd bought a piece of sand dune or swampland with no roads, no water, no nothing. He went broke and shot himself.

There was nobody left to sue. I felt pretty disgusted, leaving the library. I got something to eat and found a pretty good place to sleep in some bushes by the freeway onramp. But twice I woke, thinking somebody was sneaking into my camp, and the second time I was too cold to go back to sleep. Lying there awake, I decided I might as well go try to find my lot anyway, since I couldn't do anything else about it until Monday.

As soon as it got light I broke camp and moved on, hitching back down the old El Camino Real with some guy hauling lettuce. He let me out on the old highway and I got my two maps out and walked along, looking for landmarks. There's creeks and estuaries still in the same places they were 70 years ago, right? And soon I'm opposite the place that was marked as a road on the map. There's no road but there is a straight line of eucalyptus trees, big old ones, going back into the brush, and I figure maybe somebody planted them along what was going to be sidewalk. I step off the highway and follow them in.

Well, there ain't no sidewalk, that's for damn sure, there's water and cattails and black mud, and here and there sort of islands of black walnut and willow scrub. And poison oak, all right, bright red. Did you see it? You have to watch out, man. Before I go ten feet in, I can't hear the noise of the highway behind me anymore.

But as I'm going in, measuring out the distance so I can find my lot, I'm noticing there's crawdaddies in the mud and blackberry bushes and I'm hearing ducks or something quacking not too far off and I'm thinking, "Fuck, this isn't so bad; I could camp here, if I could find a dry place". And I can see ahead the tops of these high sand dunes. I know the ocean's just the other side and there's got to be fish and mussels and stuff, right?

And it served me right that I wasn't watching out, because he almost got me.

But I did have my hunting knife drawn, at least, I wasn't totally dumb, and it happened way fast. I opened up that big artery under the ribcage. He went back like a bundle of dry sticks when I pushed him away and I saw he was an old *old* dude, skin like paper, and his long hair and beard were snow-white. I felt bad. But he had a bayonet in his hand and he was trying to do the same to me, you know?

He sort of smiled at me before he bled out. That was something, anyway.

You want some more? Sure, have the rest of the bottle. Packs a wallop, don't it? Anyway. I cleaned my knife and looked around.

I was in this clearing, right here, which coincidentally was just about where my property line should be. There were willows all around the edge and one hanging down yellow leaves. It was so, so quiet. Still is. Listen: You can't hear the ocean. You can't hear the highway. Hell, you can't even hear the wind. But this was my land, and it was dry, and I thought maybe I could build myself a cabin or something.

I stood real still and looked around, and pretty soon I could spot where the old dude had had his camp. He'd hidden it all pretty well. There weren't even any footprints. But back under a bush he'd stashed an old ammo box with a rolled-up hammock in it with some bottles of aspirin and a tin mug, and a bowl and a fork and spoon, and a can opener. Fanning out from there, hidden under a couple of stained old canvas tarps that had the best camouflage paint job I'd ever seen, he had a cache of canned food and another with some cans of oil and a cook pot. The strangest thing was this big old bronze bowl, and the inside was all blackened. It took me a while to figure out that that was his fire-bowl. He built his campfires in it, see? You put it out every morning, dump the ashes down the latrine, and there's no trace.

And you couldn't have spotted any of this stuff, standing here, even though it was none of it more than ten yards away. You'd have to be somebody like me, to find it at all. I had to hand it to the old guy. The more I thought about it, the more I started thinking he must have been a soldier too.

I hauled his body over into the clearing and searched him. He had on all this old stained and faded shit that looked like he'd scrounged it out of dumpsters. And oh, man, he was old. His boots were way too small for me and pretty worn out so I left them on him, but along with the bayonet he had a beautiful old gun in a holster that had just shaped itself around it like a second skin, leather like butter. It was kind of rank from his armpit but you could tell he'd taken care of it every day of his life. There were also a couple of knives in his boots and a key on a string around his neck, a little key like for a trunk or a locker.

I knew the ammo box didn't lock, so I figured he had to have another cache someplace around there. It took me an hour to find it; it was off under a willow tree. There were three rocks lined up against the trunk. I dug down about a foot under them and found a kind of box he'd made of slabs of rock, and inside it was the lockbox. It was wooden; had this old-fashioned writing across it that said *"Souvenir of the Redwoods"*, sort of flaking off and hard to read, and a painted flower which I guess was supposed to be a California poppy. The lock was a little rusty but the key fit, and I got it open.

It was like my mom's trunk again. There were some old letters written in brown ink, and an old brown photo of a girl and another of a kid in a uniform. There were some medals. That was when I got this sort of sick feeling. And then I found his honorable discharge papers. And then his hospital paperwork. That old guy was a veteran of the Spanish American War. He'd maybe come out to the tuberculosis clinic and got cured, but he never went home. I'm not ashamed to tell you I fucking cried like a baby. And I was sooo glad I hadn't taken his ears.

If only he hadn't rushed me, you know? We could have talked. I wanted to ask him about his war and tell him about mine. He'd have known where my head was at, maybe only him in the whole world, because I never could tell Darla about it and it was just a job to the doctor at the psych clinic.

But now he was, like, ninety pounds of dead meat. So I went back and I buried him, right there on my land, nice and deep, but with respect, and I sang Taps. That's an American hero buried there, man. That's why I keep the flag drawn on there and the edges lined out with clamshells.

What'd I do with the wooden box? I put it back, man, what did you think I'd do with it? I added all my own stuff to it, too, my deed and my discharge papers and everything. And I sat there and did some thinking.

If the old dude had been able to hide out there for 70 years or however long it was, there was no reason I couldn't too. I didn't need to go back into San Luis and argue with the County or the Park Service or whoever. I could live here on my land. I wasn't going to build any cabins or shit like that, because doing that would be like putting up a fucking neon sign saying *Here I Am*, but I remembered how to live in the jungle real good. And the old dude had never forgotten how, that was easy to see.

It's kind of like a jungle, anyway. The black mud smells the same. The trees are different and there aren't tigers, but there's cougars and bobcats, and there's enough of their smell in the air to keep you sharp. You learn so good that when a stranger comes through you can pick up their smell on the wind the second they step off the highway. Yeah, I smelled *you*. I saw you coming, believe me.

And…when I'd got over feeling bad about the killing, I actually began to feel pretty good. I came back from Nam and coming home was like I was dreaming, but I knew nothing was real, it was *nice* but it wasn't real. There was Darla and the house and her flowers and kids playing in the park, people in their cars, songs on the radio, everybody thinking they're all safe and happy, but I knew I was going to wake up. And now I had. The dream was over and it was a relief, you know what I mean? And I knew that was why the old dude had never gone home either. He'd woken up.

I settled in real fast. I found the well he dug, way out toward the dunes, where he'd sunk an old iron pot with the bottom rusted out. The water made me a little sick at first, but I got used to it. I found his trails—you wouldn't be able to see them, but I knew what to look for. Places where the bole of a snag stump looks polished, from boots rubbing it as they pass. Branches broken in a certain way. Leaves flattened out.

I quit smoking, cold turkey. Waste of money and anyway that's one of the easiest ways to get caught, you know? The smell of tobacco and the smoke giving away your location. Three on a match, that's bad luck, and they say it's because it takes the first two guys before the sniper can draw a bead on the flame, but really any good sniper can get you as soon as you light up. The Viet Cong sure could. And anyway I needed money to buy canned food for the winters, after I'd cleaned out the old dude's cache.

Foraging was easy, in summer. Plenty to eat around here. I found out about the clams and if you go two miles out that way, there's the spinach fields and they got lettuce, artichokes, broccoli too. I already knew enough to drag a branch with leaves behind me, to rub out my tracks, and never to sleep in the same place two nights running. Sometimes I'd be stringing up the hammock in a willow clump or a walnut tree and I'd find shiny places on just the right branches, and I knew the old dude had slept here too.

And, you know, when you wake up back here in the night, there's nobody to tell you you're crazy, to say there's nobody coming up the stairs, to say everything is all right when you know fucking well everything *isn't* all right.

The enemy is out there in the night. Or somebody is. Something is. Always. We all know it, way back in our little monkey brains, and we pile layers of shit on top of the truth, books and music and laws, so we can pretend it isn't so. But people die, every day, because they thought they were safe.

The jungle is everywhere and she's the hardest bitch you'll ever meet. She doesn't give a shit about you and she'll kill you the minute you screw up, but you go to her because you can't go anywhere else. She's the only real thing there is.

So I defended my jungle. For a while, I just thought I had park rangers to watch out for. And now and then somebody like you would come back here, looking for a place to get stoned maybe, huh? Clowns from the Recreational Area, trespassing. Wandering over from the campground. It's a good campground. I find a lot of good stuff in the dumpsters there. Bottles you can take up to some of the liquor stores off the highway, and turn in for the deposit. You don't want to go to the same one twice, though. Or any of them too often.

Yeah, it's hot, huh? Lot of flies in the summer. It's a little better in the winter. The third year I was here we had rain like you wouldn't believe. The water level rose and I had to take to the trees. Even way up in the branches, I found where the old guy had carved his name. It was all grown over with bark, so he must have done it years back. I guess he thought nobody would ever see it but him. Maybe he needed to look at his name now and then, to remember who he was. I don't know. I caught bronchitis that year, almost thought I'd die. Cured myself by stripping down to my shorts and walking out on the beach when there was sun, letting the heat bake through me. I got too nervous, though, trying to pass as one of them. It felt unreal.

And I didn't like being away from here that long, either.

Why? Because I'm supposed to be here. And because of the ambushes. How you feeling now, buddy?

See, what I ought to have expected, after the way the old guy jumped me, was that somebody else would come along and try to do the same. And somebody did. It took a year, but somebody did.

He must have been watching me a couple of days, because he knew when I went to the latrine and where it was. See, if it had been me, I'd have jumped him while he had his pants down, but he waited and jumped out of a tree as I was coming back. That tree right there. But I knew he was there by that time, I could smell him. Guy about my age, wearing cammies new from a surplus store, the idiot. He had the soot smeared under his eyes and the headband and the whole nine yards. Playing soldier, I guess.

He didn't make a sound and neither did I. In fact nothing made any sound. There was the kind of silence that pushes against your eardrums, you know what I'm saying? I learned right then to listen for that soundless kind of air. The jungle's holding her breath.

He was heavier than me but I was faster. And stronger. He had some karate moves, which I didn't, but I don't think he'd ever really been in combat. I broke his wrist getting his knife away from him. It took a long time…

His boots were brand new and my size but worthless to me, with those big old tire patterns on the soles. I found his tracks afterward all over the trail, but I hadn't noticed because I'd been staying in the clearing for a couple of days. I learned better.

What'd I do with him? Hung him up and bled him into the latrine, and then dragged him out to where the dunes start. There's a field that's being eaten by the sand, bit by bit, losing a couple feet every year. I put him six feet down under the edge and by a month later he was under twenty feet of dune. The old dude must have gotten rid of his kills the same way, because I've never found any of his. Did I honor Mr. Cammie? Hell no. No American flags for that guy. He was a fucking amateur. And a civilian.

It's gotten so I can tell, now, when they come through. The air changes. The light changes. The air shines and it's so quiet.

I see her sometimes afterward. She's smiling at me. Her hair is leaves with the moon in them, her skin is colors hard to see. Her teeth are sharp. She's happy with me.

See that branch up there? That yellow one. The first year I was here I thought it was just early frost in that one place or something, but it stayed like that even in winter, after all the other leaves had fallen. Stayed like that even when the catkins and the little green leaves came on the other branches in spring. It never changes.

Did you finish high school, dude? No?... I had a good education, myself. St. Ignatius Loyola High School. A big library there, man.

Anyway. The air starts to change. Everything goes all quiet and I know he's coming. Sometimes I have a whole hour before somebody comes walking through my trees. I'm always waiting. Oh, no, he's different every time. And I know why it's so quiet, why I couldn't hear the highway anymore even if some asshole was out there blasting on his truck horn. *The highway isn't there then.*

I went out once, just to see. I went past the last eucalyptus tree and waded out a little, but I couldn't see any pavement or hear any cars. The world out there had just vanished. Swear to God. I thought it might be the fog but it wasn't, there was nothing dripping from the trees, the air was dry as the desert, dreamlike. I stood there staring and staring, and listening and listening, and nearly got myself killed, because the guy just came walking out of the nothingness with a kind of dazed expression on his face, but I'd let him see me. And he almost nailed me right there. See this? He did that. It still hurts, after all these years, when a storm's blowing in. I've still got the spearhead, in one of my caches.

That was what I said, *spearhead*. A bronze one. Because, see, sometimes it's a guy in cammies, but sometimes it's a guy in rags. And once it was a kid in a blue woolen uniform. There have been some other uniforms too. That was when I started to figure it out. The jungle is outside of things like time…But you really don't know what that yellow branch means, do you? Because you're just some dumbass stoner with no education.

Listen to me, man; this is sacred ground. This is *her* place, the jungle. There was a reason I found my way here. It was part of the plan. There was a reason for everything, there was a reason why nothing else in my life ever worked out.

We all start out to serve her, all of us, and that's why your dad beats the living crap out of you when you're a kid, it's why the upperclassmen fuck with you, it's why the drill sergeant calls you a maggot and a pussy and makes you do pushups until you vomit. It's why they ship you off into the jungle to kill. It's to weed out the unfit ones.

If I'd been a paper boy like Mom wanted, if I'd listened to Father James and the line he tried to sell me, if I'd been able to sleep nights with Darla and get a nice job as a grocery store boxboy like she wanted and pay rent and walk the line and pretend it was all normal—I'd have been unfit too. But I couldn't. Because I always knew it was all crap. I was always headed for this place, back in the trees.

This is the only place that's real. This is where the Truth is. And once you *know* the Truth you'll find your way here, sooner or later, and you'll fight, and if you aren't fit for the job you'll lose. I'm her priest, now. There's only ever one at a time.

I patrol her jungle and I keep it real. There's no bullshit here. No dreaming. Anybody comes in and profanes her place gets killed, as long as I'm strong enough, fast enough, smart enough. Like the old dude before me. And some get sacrificed.

Look up at that yellow branch, man. What do you think those are, tied all along between the golden leaves, huh? Take a good guess. Trespasser.

Look at you, crying and whimpering like a goddam little girl. Like I'd fight you! I wouldn't dirty my knife on you, not the knife I killed the old dude with. He was a king and a hero, and you're…a coward. Thinking you'd score my little stash of nickels and dimes. A maggot thief.

A trespassing maggot.

My knife is only for warriors.

You didn't really think that was Everclear you were drinking, did you?

86 DEATHDICK ROAD

JEFFREY FORD

I **HAD** on my good pants, the uncomfortable ones, and was in the car with Lynn. I knew we were going somewhere I didn't have any interest in going, because I was wearing a tie and jacket. She had on the lemon perfume I'd bought her two Christmases back.

"When was the last time we were out on a date?" she said. She wore a brightly colored shawl, paisley in gold and orange. It came to me that her hair, when I wasn't noticing, had gotten longer, the way she'd worn it back in college.

"Long time," I said, and made the turn on 206, heading south. Twilight was giving way to a cool spring night, and we drove with the windows open. "Who told you about this guy?" I asked.

"I saw Theda in the market Wednesday. She and Joe went to see him. She said the guy's amazing."

"The Man Who Knew Too Much?" I asked.

"No, he's The Smartest Man in the World."

"But, come on, fifty bucks to behold his brilliance..." I said and sighed through my nose.

"Don't be insipid," she said. "You can ask him anything and he knows the answer."

"I could stay home and get that on the internet for free," I said.

Her smile went to a straight line. Before things could get rotten, I said, "How many questions do you get to ask?" It was all I could think of.

"Everybody gets one question," she said, staring through the windshield.

"What are you going to ask him?"

"Why you're such a turd," she said.

"What did Theda ask him? 2+2?"

"She asked him if she was ever going to have a kid."

"It doesn't take the smartest man in the world to answer that one," I said. "She's 50 if she's a day."

"He told her, 'No,' but after he gave his answer, she said he got up from his throne and walked over to her table. He shook hands with Joe, and then leaning over Theda, the smartest man in the world cupped her left breast with his right hand and whispered, 'Know this.' She said she felt a spark inside her that went straight to her brain and exploded—that's what she said. She started crying, the audience clapped, the guy returned to his throne and took the next question."

"*Know what?*" I asked.

"I don't know," said Lynn and laughed.

We drove on, listening to the radio, neither of us saying much except for me wondering aloud if there was going to be any booze involved.

Lynn gave a curt, "No," and then said, "OK, you have to slow down here. We have to look for a dirt road, going into the trees up on the left."

"What's the address?" I asked, easing down on the brake.

She lifted a piece of paper off her lap and unfolded it quickly. Turning on the overhead light, she read, "86 Deathdick Road."

Suddenly I was almost past the entrance in the trees. I slammed on the brakes. There was no other traffic behind us, so I backed up a little and made the turn.

"OK, look for Deathdick," she said.

"Are you kidding? Deathdick?" I said. I didn't see any streets, just the dirt road ahead, winding through the woods, lit by my headlights.

"The place is called *Mullions*," she said.

I looked over at Lynn, and her hair was glowing. When I looked back at the road, we were driving on asphalt through a posh suburban neighborhood of McMansions and landscaped lawns. Up ahead, I saw a lot of cars parked along the street on both sides.

"I guess that's it," I said.

"But which house?" asked Lynn.

I slowed way down and crept to the end of the car line on the right hand curb. We got out and I joined her on the sidewalk. Lynn pointed to the front lawn two doors down at a bright tube of violet neon twisted into the name *Mullions*.

"Is this place legal?" I asked.

"I guess so," she said.

We were met at the front door by a thin woman on the down side of sixty. She wasn't fooling anyone with the surgical cinching of her face. "Millions to Mullions," she said. "I'm Jenny. I hope you're ready for some answers tonight." She flashed us a smile of giant teeth and held out her hand, palm up.

Lynn dug through her purse and retrieved our fifty. Once Jenny had it in her hand, she said, "Ask well," and then stepped aside as we passed into the living room.

Once we were out of earshot, Lynn said, "What was up with her face?"

"It's better to ask well than look well," I said.

The living room was packed, people milling around, talking, sitting on the gold, upholstered furniture. A huge bad painting of a garden with a waterfall and a McMansion in the background hung in an ornate frame in the center of the wall above the couch. The carpet was also gold, and there was a small chandelier above. I looked around, and right off the bat, I spotted some of my neighbors from town.

I pointed out Dornsberry to Lynn and she rolled her eyes and whispered, "Not that douche bag." I'd never seen this guy at a party in town that he wasn't lecturing some poor bastard on the finer points of golf. A holy-rolling, cigar-smoking runt. His presence was bad enough, but off to the left of us was Mrs. Krull, laying out for some old guy on the verge of either sleep or death one of her long bummer stories. When her one-legged aunt had succumbed to cancer of the vagina, she'd called and kept me on the phone for an hour with the excruciating details. I'd heard she had a pair of gray parrots on perches in her dining room that crapped willy nilly and constantly repeated the phrase, "Just kill me," in her husband's voice.

Lynn saw I'd noticed Krull, and she said, "Sorry."

"This smartest man better be really smart," I said. Then a woman walked by carrying a small plate with hors-d'oeuvres on it. I thought I caught a glimpse of pigs-in-a-blanket. "Eats," I said.

"If they have anything to drink beside soda, bring me a glass," said Lynn, and I was off wending my way through the crowd, happy to have a purpose. On the way, not really knowing where I was going, I spotted a good looking young woman with a pile of blonde hair, holding a plate with water chestnuts wrapped in bacon. "Not bad," I thought, and hoped there'd be spare ribs or maybe shrimp. I got jostled by the crowd, excusing myself a dozen times for every few feet travelled. It was the sight of someone holding a beer that gave me the fortitude to continue.

Within that sea of bodies it got really hot and I started to sweat. The deep rumble of conversation washed over me from all directions, snatches of dialogue differentiating themselves for a moment and then melting back into the general hubbub. "I told her, don't try it, bitch." "Peter did so well on the SATs they had to invent a new grade for him better than A+." "The dog is old, it craps on the rug every day now." "It's supposed to snow later." When it felt as if I'd been on my pigs-in-a-blanket search for a half hour, I finally went up to a woman I vaguely recognized from the grocery store in town where she was a cashier.

"Hi, do you know where the food is?" I asked.

She shook her head, and when she did, right on the spot, she turned into Dornsberry. He gave me a look of contempt. "We're all Christians here," he said and took a long swig of his beer. "What religion are you?"

"Where'd you get the beer?" I asked.

"You've been asked a question," he said and pushed his glasses up the bridge of his nose with the back of his beer hand.

"I'm a product of the age of reason," I said. "Where's the food?"

He shook his head as if in disgust and pointed behind me. I turned around, the crowd parted, and there was a long table with bowls and plastic cups and a crystal punch bowl half filled with a yellow liquid. As I walked away from him, I heard Dornsberry hurl the insult, "Clown," at me. Any other time I might have pounded his face in, but instead I just laughed it off.

The food table, in the state I found it, held a bowl with three pretzels in it and five other bowls of a tan dip that had crusted dark brown at the edges. A live fly buzzed in the middle of one bowl, unable to free itself.

"That'll be a fossil some day," said a voice behind me. I turned to see a thin man in a black tuxedo. He had a wave of slick dark hair in front, big clunky, black-framed glasses and a thinly trimmed mustache.

"Pretty appetizing, huh?" I said to him.

"Allow me to introduce myself," he said. "I'm the smartest man in the world."

I shook his hand and told him my name. "If you're the smartest man in the world," I said, "how'd you wind up here?"

He gave a wry smile and told me, "I only answer questions for money."

I felt in my pants pockets for a crumpled bill. Taking it out and flattening it for him, I said, "Five bucks if you can tell me where I can get a beer."

"Five won't do it," he said. Now he had on a top hat and a cape and looked like Mandrake the Magician with glasses. "But five will get you half an answer."

I handed him the bill. "I'll take it," I said.

"You've got to go through the kitchen, that way," he said and pointed. "Once you're there, go out the side door onto the patio. That's all I can afford to tell you."

"A steep price for some pretty thin shit," I said to him, and couldn't believe I was getting belligerent with the smartest man in the world. There was something exhilarating about it.

"When your wife asks her question later," he said, "after I answer it, I'm going to kiss her and slip her the tongue so deeply I'll taste her panties. She'll see god, my friend." He tipped back his top hat and laughed arrogantly.

I picked up a crusted bowl of dip. "Touch my wife and you'll be the deadest man in the world," I said. Then I threw the bowl at him. He ducked at the last second, and the bowl flew into the face of a heavy-set older woman in a sequined gown behind him. Tan goo dripped from her jowls and the bowl hit the wooden floor and shattered. For a moment, I wondered where the carpet had gone. The woman I hit had been standing with an aged gentleman wearing a military uniform and sporting ridiculously thick mutton chop side burns. "Preposterous," he shouted and his monocle fell from his eye. He reached for the sword he had in a scabbard at his side. Meanwhile the smartest man in the world had lived up to his name for once and had split. I didn't see him anywhere. I followed his lead and merged into the crowd, moving fast, sweating profusely.

In the kitchen, there was a fire eater. He was performing in the corner by the range. People had gathered around to watch and it was impossible to get through to the patio door, which I could glimpse occasionally between heads in the crowd. I had to wait for him to finish his act and hope the logjam broke up.

I watched him. He had two little torches that he held with the middle finger of his right hand. He'd pour lighter fluid on them and then turn on the range and light them off the burner. He had a small blonde pony tail and a beat up face, broken nose and scar tissue around the eyes. He was a lackluster showman. His approach was to say, "I'm gonna eat fire now," in a low, placid voice, and then he ate it.

After you've seen someone eat fire once, there's not much else to it. I watched him eat fire five times, and by the fourth time, even though nobody left, nobody was clapping either. I had cold beer on my mind, so, after the fifth time, I said in a loud voice, "Alright, let's get on with it." To my surprise, people started leaving the kitchen. The Fire Eater tried to see who'd said it, but I kept my gaze down and pushed gently forward.

I found the cooler of beer out on the patio. It was filled with ice and Rolling Rock. I took one and sat down at a glass topped table, on a wrought iron chair with arms my fat ass barely fit between. I was alone out there in the dark. The night was cool but pleasant, and I could feel the sweat drying. Someone had left behind a pack of cigarettes, Lucky Strikes (I didn't know they still made them) and a lighter. That beer tasted like heaven, and the cig wasn't far behind. I took out my cell phone and dialed Lynn.

It rang and rang, and then she answered. "Where are you?" she said.

I told her, "I'm out on the patio, having a beer."

"The show's going to start any minute," she said. "I got us a table."

"You can't believe how big the place is," I said. "How many people are here. It took me forever to get to the food table."

"Bring me a beer," she said.

"Will do. And listen, if I don't get back in time and the smartest man in the world answers your question, don't let him touch you." There was silence from the other end of the line. I said her name a couple times, but it was clear we'd either been cut off or she'd thought we were through and hung up.

I put the cigarettes and lighter in one jacket pocket, and then took another beer and put that in my other jacket pocket. I put my smoke out in a planter at the edge of the patio and then turned to head back in. As I moved toward the house, I saw the smartest man in the world's face at the window of the door. He smiled at me and waved before looking down as if he was going to open it and come out. An instant later he was gone. I tried the door knob and realized, what he'd done was lock it. When I knocked on the door, I looked inside and saw the kitchen was completely empty.

I heard a window opening above me on the second floor. I backed onto the patio and looked up. The smartest man in the world poked his head out. He was again wearing his top hat. "Perhaps like in Chaucer's Miller's Tale you can climb up here and kiss my hairy ass," he said.

"Let me in," I said.

"There's a reason they call me the smartest man in the world," he said. "The show starts in ten minutes."

"I'm going to call the cops," I told him.

"Dornsberry says you're a pussy," said the smartest man.

"I'll kill you both," I shouted.

"No you won't. Now hurry around front and pay again to be let in. You might catch me answering your wife's question." I heard Dornsberry's laughter in the background. The window shut with a bang.

I took out my cell phone, but when I flipped it open it was dead. "Shit," I said, and headed for the edge of the patio. Only then did I notice that the side of the house butted up against the edge of a forest. In the moonlight I could make out tall pine trees in both directions. There was a path that went either around the back of the place through the trees or one that looked like it led to the front of the house. I was just about to head for the front when I realized that was the smartest man's advice. What were the chances he was going to tell me the best way to go? I stepped onto the path and headed toward the back. There were stretches of perfect night where the pines blocked the moon completely.

I walked fast for a ways, but was soon out of breath and my Achilles tendon was aching, so I slowed down. Just then I noticed something on the side of the path, like a lectern. I stepped over to it. It was a chest high stand with a plaque on top situated at an angle. There was something written on it. I took out the lighter, flicked it, and quickly read the plaque. It said—*Beware of Owls!* **Mullions** *Is Not Responsible For Any Damages Or Deaths Caused By Owls.*

I flicked the lighter again, and this time noticed that beneath the writing there was an etching of a large owl in mid-flight, grasping in its talons the severed head of Jenny, the Mullions' hostess. "Killer owls?" I said aloud. A stiff breeze blew the flame out and it felt more like autumn than spring. I noticed the path was strewn with fallen leaves. "That's ridiculous," I said, and started walking again. Two minutes later, I wrapped my hand around the neck of the beer bottle in my pocket and took it out to use as a club.

"Fuck those owls," I told myself, "I have to get back to Lynn." I put on as much steam as I could manage, and with almost every step, the tendon in my left heel got worse. "She'll never let him touch her," I said to myself. "If he tries, she'll punch him in the face and break his glasses." I hobbled a few more yards, and then thought, "Or will she?"

That's when I happened to look up and notice the pairs of yellow eyes trimming the trees like dull Christmas lights. They were everywhere. My knees went weak and my heart began to pound so hard I could hear it in my right ear. I desperately wanted to run but knew I wouldn't get far. Instead, I crept forward, trembling, praying they hadn't noticed me and wouldn't. In whispers, like a novena, I recited the theme song to the afternoon television cartoon of my youth, Tobor, The Eighth Man.

I got only as far as, "The F.B.I. is helpless. It's forty stories tall," when a shrill screech tore through the dark. An owl's flight is silent, but I heard the beating of their wings in my mind as they swooped after me. The breeze picked up and I pushed against it, trying to run, waving the beer bottle over my head and ducking. It was like running through water. I felt their talons at my back and what hair I have. Feathers whipped my cheeks. I tried to scream but it came forth, a long, breathy fart.

Just when I thought I was finished I collided with another person on the path, and for some reason the owls miraculously retreated. I lit the lighter to see who it was, and only when I saw it was Mrs. Krull did I realize she'd been talking the whole time. There was a glassy vacant stare to her froggy eyes. Her lips were moving and she was in the midst of the story of her one legged aunt. I gathered my wits, walking alongside of her, and said, "Mrs. Krull, what are you doing out here?" She moved steadily forward, staring straight ahead as if in a trance. All the time the words spilled out of her.

It came to me not as a thought but as a feeling that it was precisely her grim tale that kept the owls at bay. They were above us and to the sides everywhere, but they didn't stir from their perches. Occasionally one would hoot in the distance, a feather would fall, but they wouldn't attack. When she was finishing up the story of her aunt's demise, for the first time in my life, I hoped she had another one ready.

There was a mere half a breath pause before the next pathetic tale was born. She spoke about a couple she knew from her old neighborhood. Nice people. They had three kids. They all went on a vacation upstate New York. They drove all day and into the night. Here, she went into the details of the family and time seemed to pass in a whirl before I again picked up the thread of the story with the father pulling over on the side of the road to take a piss. They were on the interstate. He got out, told his wife he'd be right back, and then mounting a small hill, disappeared over the top.

"Some time passed," said Mrs. Krull. "The wife started wondering, how long will my husband piss for? Finally, after almost 20 minutes, she told the kids she'd be right back and to stay in the car. She went to look for her husband. Up the hill she went in the dark. The kids were alone in the car and probably eventually got scared when their mother didn't return."

I noticed that all around us, as Mrs. Krull ground out her story with relentless persistence, the owls were keeling off their branches and falling to the forest floor. I knew in my heart that it was my neighbor's tragic droning that rendered them insensate. "Right over the rise of that small hill, unbeknownst to him and her, was the edge of a cliff. Both hadn't seen the edge in the dark and fallen 200 feet to their deaths," she said.

The owls fell like pillows; hit the ground with muffled thuds. Every now and then there was a weak squawk. "Then the kids," said Mrs. Krull, "one after the other. First the oldest, a boy, Kenneth, who was in my Robert's grade (he was a mean spirited kid), and then the middle one, the sister, she was adorable. They each went looking in their turn and each fell to their deaths. They probably screamed in terror but no one heard them. Maybe they landed on their parents, but it still killed them."

Mrs. Krull's story was making even me dizzy. It appeared that she had subdued the owls, so I worked up the courage to escape her. "Then the last child, little Freddie, I have a photo of him in shorts and a collar shirt with a small bow tie. I could just bite those cheeks. He went next up the hill in the dark. But he was my little genius and figured out what had happened. He ran to get help."

"Well, at least little Freddie made it," I said, and veered away from Mrs. Krull, right off the path and directly into the trees. At the moment, I didn't care where I was going. I stumbled in a rut between two trees, still light headed. The last thing I heard Krull say as I groped blindly through the underbrush was, "He ran out onto the highway to flag down a car, and the driver didn't see him till it was too late."

I tramped unsteadily forward, kicking downed owl carcasses, like empty birthday piñatas, out of my way. Mrs. Krull's sad bullshit had sucked their life. It struck me that the potential of her drivel was like a terrible super power, and I had a brief vision of her walking through the sky on a blue day, dressed in white robes with a halo, a six foot, uprooted sun flower chained to her ankle, gliding along behind her.

It was a fear soaked hour or more, submerged in the dark, skinning my shins, taking branches to the face, before I returned to the patio. Sitting in the wrought iron chair at the table, I popped the beer I'd been carrying and lit up a smoke. I noticed that the house was perfectly silent and dark.

"I missed the whole god damn thing," I thought. "I never got to ask my question, Lynn has long been tongue kissed by the smartest man in the world and seen god, and I'm castaway in Owl Forest. What the fuck?"

After finishing the cigarette and half the beer, I got up and checked the kitchen door. To my surprise and elation, it was unlocked. I opened it and stepped into the silence of the dark house. Without even closing the door behind me, I was off on a beeline for the front door. Who knows how long it took to cross the kitchen, to reach the entrance to the living room, which, itself, was vast. Only when passing the occasional window did the moonlight allow me to see where I was going. Otherwise, I slammed against furniture and at one point might have tripped over a body.

My tendon was acting up badly, so I stopped after a long while by one of the windows and had another smoke. While I rested, I looked outside and saw that it was snowing. As soon as I saw the snow, I heard the wind howl. "Great," I said. I put the cigarette out on the windowsill and left it there. No more than a dozen limping steps later, I collided with the edge of the food table and got a thrill to know I was making progress. A little ways after that I saw small intermittent bursts of flame in the distance.

That flame was my lighthouse. For some reason I believed it would bring me to the front door and my escape. So entranced was I with the rhythmic fire that grew ever more prominent with each painful step that I was almost upon the source of the phenomenon before I realized what was causing it. The scene suddenly materialized out of the dark no more than six feet in front of me.

There was Jenny, completely naked, her sagging yet emaciated body perched in the throne of the smartest man in the world with her legs spread and hooked over its wooden arms. Kneeling in front of her was the Fire Eater with his head between her legs, only this time it wasn't fire he was eating. I watched as Jenny glowed from inside like a jack 'o lantern, saw the silhouettes of her ribs and spine and heart. Then she gave a slight moan, opened her mouth and a burst of flame shot out. I took a step back and stared in amazement.

I was afraid they'd see me there, but I was also afraid to move. Finally, I don't know what possessed me, it was like some kind of momentary insanity, I yelled, "I see you." The Fire Eater never even turned around but kept working like he was non-union. Jenny lifted herself a little and turned to look at me. She reached up to her chin and then grabbing it, literally pulled her face off like it was a rubber mask. The jaws of her skull head creaked open. There came a moan and then she shot a long burst of fire at me. I ran, but felt the sting of her flaming tongue on my left earlobe.

The next thing I knew, I was standing out on the front lawn. It was freezing and the snow was driving down. I passed the neon Mullions sign, no longer lit, on my way to the street. Heading in the direction Lynn and I had initially come, I shivered, huddled inside my suit jacket, the collar flipped up and doing nothing for me. I had no idea where I was or how to get home, and there was a considerable chance I might freeze to death.

In my desperation I was going to give my phone one more try, and when I looked down, I saw Lynn's shawl half covered in the drifting snow. I picked it up and put it to my face. On a sunny Halloween 32 years ago, we took a bottle of tequila and climbed a mountain. At the top there was a rundown shack. Inside there was a metal bed frame, a three legged chair with a frayed wicker seat fallen in the corner, and a warped desk with a rash of pale fungus. Dead leaves and brittle news pages littered the floor. The door hung by one hinge; there was broken glass beneath the single window. In a drawer of the desk, Lynn found a mildewed dictionary and in it a letter from 1932. The envelope was marked Return To Sender. The salutation read—*Love you forever.*

A car came slowly down the road toward me and when it drew close, its head lights flicked on and off. It drew up next to me, a late model Mercedes. The window went down, a cloud of cigar smoke escaped, and I saw it was Dornsberry. "Get in," he said. "The owls are waking up." For just a second, I was going to tell him to fuck off, but the promise of owls, not to mention the bitter cold, humbled me. I hobbled around to the passenger side and got in.

"Are you going to town?" I asked him.

"Yeah, I'll drop you at your place."

The car was so warm and it felt great to get off my feet. "I ran into the owls earlier," I said.

Dornsberry's cigar had vanished. Both his black gloved hands were on the leather steering wheel. He seemed affable, like some whole different Dornsberry I'd never met. "I told Jenny," he said, "you gotta poison those fucking owls. What a liability. I told her what eats owls? Get some of that. Like weasels or something. Maybe a wolf ... whatever."

"They seem put off by Mrs. Krull," I said.

"Well, nobody said they were stupid," said Dornsberry. "They're just mean as hell. I was back in the forest tonight, scared out of my wits they'd catch me. I've been bitten by those things before. Luckily, for some reason, every one of the little bastards was knocked out. I stole two of their eggs." He reached into his pocket with his right hand and brought out a large brown egg. "Take this one," he said.

What the hell, I took it and put it in my pocket. "Thanks," I said.

"Each time it lays, every she-owl drops two eggs, no more no less. It is said that if you place one of these eggs in the hand of a sleeping woman, she will tell you only the truth. Have her hold the other, though, and she will tell only lies."

"Where'd you hear that?" I asked.

"The smartest man in the world told me," he said.

Just his name set me off. I had a thing or two to say to Dornsberry about the smartest man, but before I could launch into it, he said, "Here's your place."

I looked out the window and saw my house, a snow drift going halfway up the front steps. The sight of it almost brought tears to my eyes. I opened the door and got out. "Thanks," I called back, and shut the door. I took a single step when I heard the passenger window slide down. Turning to see what was up, I caught a glimpse of Dornsberry flipping me the bird. "You're such a pussy," he said, revved the engine and tried to peel out in the snow. The car shot off down the street sideways on the ice, righted itself for a moment and then crashed into the light pole on the corner.

The lights were out in our bedroom. Lynn was in bed asleep. She lay on her side, her hair not so long anymore, right arm sticking out from beneath the covers. With the greatest care I eased down on the edge of the mattress next to her. I sat for a time with my eyes closed and then carefully placed the owl egg in her right hand.

"Did you ask the smartest man in the world your question?" I whispered.

Perhaps a half a minute passed before she murmured, "Yes."

"Did he answer it?" I asked.

"Yes," she finally said.

"Did he kiss you?"

"Yes."

"What was it like?"

"His tongue was like four hot dogs."

"Did you see god?"

"No, I saw you, stumbling through the dark forest, lost."

"What was your question?" I asked.

"If you still loved me."

"And what was his answer?"

"He said his answer had two parts. The first part was—Yes, and for the second part he got off his throne and kissed me."

I almost didn't ask it, but finally I said, "Are you in love with the smartest man in the world?"

"Yes," she said.

I took the egg out of her hand and got up. For a long time, I stood by the bedroom window, staring into the dark at the falling snow, listening to the screech of the wind. "After all these years," I said, and then spotted, out on the street in front of the house, a figure trudging by. It was too dark for me to make out the form, but when the egg shattered in my hand, I knew it must be Mrs. Krull. I vowed to become the smartest man in the world as the yolk dripped through my fingers.